MALLORY
IN
FULL
COLOR

Also by Elisa Stone Leahy

Tethered to Other Stars

MALLORY
IN
FULL
COLOR

ELISA STONE LEAHY

Quill Tree Books
An Imprint of HarperCollinsPublishers

Quill Tree Books is an imprint of HarperCollins Publishers.

Mallory in Full Color
Text copyright © 2024 by Elisabeth Leahy
Illustrations copyright © 2024 by Maine Diaz

Library of Congress Control Number: 2023948455
ISBN 978-0-06-325553-1

Typography by David DeWitt
24 25 26 27 28 LBC 5 4 3 2 1

First Edition

To anyone of any age still searching for who you are. May you have access to a full palette of colors as you discover the ever-changing, multifaceted miracle of your own identity.

And to Matthew, who loves me in all my many shades, even those neither of us expected.

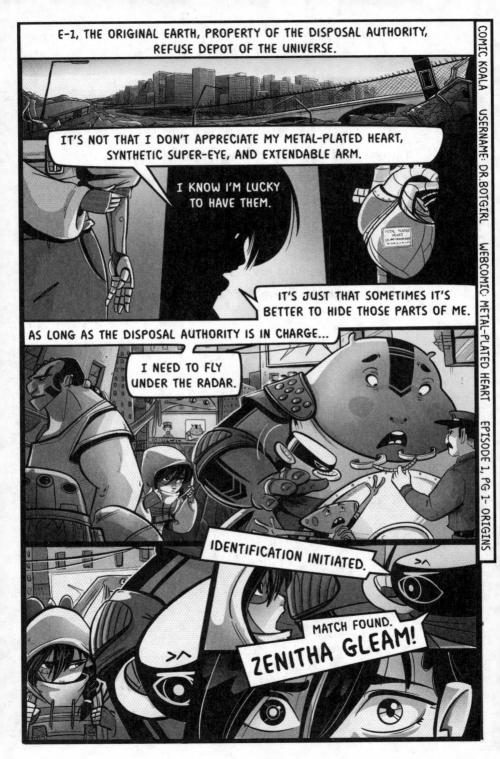

Chapter One

"MALLORY MARSH!"

Mal jumped, her pencil scratching a jagged line through Zee's cyborg face. She leaned forward in her seat, hiding the sketchbook in her lap and smiling up at her teacher.

"Yes, Mr. Emerson?"

Mr. Emerson peered over his glasses at her from across the room. He had no reason to think she wasn't doing her work. She was usually the first one done with English assignments. Except for the fact that her brainstorming worksheet was lying open on top of her desk, suspiciously blank. Mal casually shifted her arm to cover the empty page. *Please don't notice*, she thought desperately. Mr. Emerson tugged at his bow tie and sniffed.

"Have you chosen a story topic already or are you still . . . brainstorming?" he asked.

Mallory glanced around the classroom. Wendy's head was bent over her notebook, her long black braid hanging over her shoulder as she tapped her pencil on the paper. Across the room Mallory could see her friend Etta with her eyes narrowed in concentration under her freshly dyed pink hair, writing furiously. Everyone but Mal was working on their story. She *had* started brainstorming. But her mind kept drifting back to the world of E-1, the futuristic Earth from her webcomic and her cyborg hero who battled the evil corporate overlords. Mal swallowed hard and lifted her knees to keep the sketchbook in place under the desk.

"Oh, um, maybe," Mal said. "I mean, yes, I'm still brainstorming."

Mr. Emerson walked closer and Mal tried not to cringe. This was usually her best class. Mallory always felt a bit awkward about going to Leopold Preparatory Academy. LPA was a gifted school, and she wasn't a math brain like that one kid who was already taking college economics classes. Or a science brain like Wendy, who had just won the middle school science fair. But Mallory always did great in English Language Arts—until they started this unit on narrative writing and her brain decided to vacation in webcomic world.

Mr. Emerson sniffed again as he looked down at the worksheet full of questions that Mal had not answered. *Oh no.* Mallory Marsh hated letting anyone down and everything about his face said she'd let him down.

"Were my brainstorming prompts not useful to you?" he asked.

"No, they're great!" Mal said quickly. "Really . . . useful."

Mr. Emerson frowned, and Mal winced. His disappointment crawled over her skin like something alive and she couldn't help squirming in her seat. The movement sent her sketchbook sliding off her lap. It hit the floor with a thump that rang in Mal's ears like a spaceship crash-landing on a hostile planet. She froze, staring up at Mr. Emerson. His eyes narrowed behind his glasses.

"Interesting," he said, stretching the word out long and slow, like putty.

"Not as interesting as these brainstorming questions," Mal said. "You really outdid yourself on those, Mr. E. Solid handout. Excellent teachering."

Someone snort-laughed behind her, but Mal kept her gaze locked on her teacher. *Nothing to see here,* she thought desperately, sending her will out like a Jedi mind trick. *Please just walk away.*

Mr. Emerson did not walk away. He leaned down and picked up Mallory's sketchbook, peering down at the half-finished drawing. Mal held her breath. He tucked the sketchbook under his arm and walked back to the front of the room.

"Oooooh, Mal's in trouble," a kid named P.J. said. Mal wished she could glare at him. But her eyes were laser-locked on the sketchbook.

"Back to work, class," Mr. Emerson said, sliding Mal's sketchbook into a drawer in his desk. "Miss Marsh, see me after."

Wendy gave her a worried look and Mal reassured her with a smile. But the moment Wendy turned back to her work, the smile melted away. The one teacher who actually thought Mal was a good student was probably going to send her to detention. Or suspend her. Did they do that for drawing in class? Maybe now that she'd lost her top-student label, she was on a downward spiral that would end with failing ELA. And if she failed ELA she'd definitely fail everything else because ELA was her best subject. And she'd never get into college or get a job or—

A movement caught her eye. Etta was making frantic hand motions across the room, her assortment of leather bracelets dangling on her skinny wrists. Mal shot a look at Mr. Emerson, whose back was to the room while he sorted through books. Etta mouthed something, pointing at his desk. Knowing Etta she probably wanted to execute an elaborate rescue mission. Mal forced a casual smile and shook her head. The last thing she needed was Etta getting ahold of her sketchbook. Etta shrugged and bent back over her work. Mal swallowed. Getting in trouble was the absolute worst feeling and Mal knew it would cling to her all day like a bad smell. It could have been worse, though. At least Emerson hadn't looked at her sketchbook too closely.

Mal watched Mr. Emerson's fingers flip the pages of her sketchbook one by one, his eyes following each page like he was scanning them into his memory. She thought she might be sick.

"It's not that this isn't an interesting concept," Mr. Emerson said, examining a scene where Zee uses her cyborg arm extension to save an alien cat. "It is creative."

It took everything Mal had to keep from reaching out a hand to stop him from turning the page. She shot a quick glance around, relieved that none of the kids leaving the classroom were close to her teacher's desk. No one in real life had ever seen these sketches.

"But it's really not a narrative. Not in the sense we are looking for in this class," Mr. Emerson continued, squinting down at a sketch of Zee's junkyard ship.

Mal blinked. *Not a narrative?* Zee had a tragic backstory and a noble mission and a character arc. There was a villain and everything. Mallory had three thousand readers on Comic Koala, for crying out loud. Not that her teacher could possibly know that. Her parents would ground her until the end of time if they ever found out she was posting her comics online.

"No?" she asked. Her voice came out in a squeak. *Stop it,* she told herself. *Don't argue with him!* Mallory Marsh didn't argue with anyone, especially teachers.

Mr. Emerson frowned. "My goal is to instruct you in writing, not comics. You have an excellent mind for story and a good grasp on narrative devices. But I'd like to see it implemented in an actual story."

Mal's mouth dropped open. He didn't think she *hadn't* been doing her assignment. He thought this *was* her assignment. And he thought it was bad. Mal's insides flip-flopped. A tiny, hidden part of her brain screamed back, *But he's wrong! It* is *an actual story!* Mal closed her mouth. She looked at her teacher and forced herself to smile.

"It was just a way to brainstorm," she said. "To help me visualize the plot."

Mr. Emerson's face cleared. "Ah, I see." He nodded. "Well, let's focus on crafting a story with words for this assignment. I do hate to see you spending your time on doodles." He closed the sketchbook and handed it back to her. "Save this for art class, Miss Marsh," he said.

The rush of relief Mal felt as she hugged her sketchbook to her chest was followed by an uncharacteristic urge to throw something. But she only widened her eyes and nodded earnestly.

"Yes, sir," she agreed. Mal was always agreeable. As she left the room, Mal slid the sketchbook carefully back into the safety of her Studio Ghibli backpack, vowing not to take any more risks. That had been much too close.

Mal had been writing webcomics for nearly two years under the name Dr.BotGirl. Technically, she couldn't post until she was thirteen so Mal had straight-up lied about her birthdate. It wasn't until she'd thought up *Metal-Plated Heart* that her subscribers had really taken off. Her main character, Zee, was a cyborg orphan living on a dystopian Earth. The Disposal Authority declares that, since Zee's body is 51 percent artificial, she is no longer human and belongs to them. But Zee escapes and fights back with a ragtag team of human and bot friends. Last month one of Mal's episodes had gone low-key viral. Fans shared screenshots on other sites and even people outside Comic Koala left comments. No one knew that the person writing sci-fi stories about a scrappy techie and her illegal AI crew sticking it to the evil polluting government was just a nerdy twelve-year-old fangirl in central Ohio. It made Mal feel powerful. But if she wanted to keep it secret, she needed to be more careful with her sketchbook.

"Did you get your notebook back?" Etta asked as Mal took a seat next to her in math class.

It's a sketch*book*, her brain corrected. But Mal kept her voice casual and answered, "Oh yeah, no big deal."

"He was seriously dictatorial about it all," Etta said, her green eyes huge. "I would have been so mad."

"What a novelty," Mal said, and Etta grinned.

Mal couldn't fathom losing her temper the way Etta did so easily, even if Mr. E had said her webcomic was *not an actual story*. A tiny thread of anger tried to crawl its way up her chest, but Mal shoved it back down.

"Don't worry," Mal said. "If I ever need to launch a campaign against a dictator, I'll call you."

"Yessss!" Etta called, raising a fist in the air.

Mal smiled. That's exactly the kind of friend Etta needed. Someone to call on her to fight injustice.

"What were you drawing in there anyway?" Etta asked.

Oh. Etta *had* noticed she was drawing. Mal shrugged and tried to look very interested in the equation Mrs. Secant was writing on the board. "Just brainstorming. Nothing major."

Deep down inside her a voice whispered that it most certainly *was* major. But no matter how much her sketches meant to her, she couldn't let anyone know. At first, it had been about online security and the age limit. But the more she wrote as Dr.BotGirl, the freer she felt. If people IRL knew about it, that would all change. Especially because all her inspiration came from the real people around her. She glanced at Etta out of the corner of her eye. Etta was too observant. She'd definitely see some similarities between herself and Smoker, the robot with the faulty personality chip who frequently lost her temper, blowing gaskets and pouring smoke from her metal frame. Mal had even updated Smoker's plating from turquoise to pink when Etta dyed her hair.

"Mallory," Jaydon whispered from behind her, "can I borrow a pencil?"

"Always," Mal said. She pulled her pencil case from her backpack. "Pick your fave."

Jaydon chose a sparkly pencil with a frog eraser. Across the aisle, Yasmin grinned.

"Mallory's magical bag," Yasmin said. "We should call you Mary Poppins."

Mal laughed. Her battered old Studio Ghibli backpack didn't look at all like Mary Poppins's carpetbag. But whatever her classmates needed, Mal usually had it. Writing utensils, first aid kit, period supplies. She had a pair of extra socks at the bottom for footwear emergencies. She'd even loaned Yasmin her new scientific calculator when hers broke the first week of school. Yasmin's maroon hijab was bent over her desk now, and Mal saw her brown fingers tapping numbers into the calculator. Even though Yasmin had offered to give it back a few times, Mal insisted she keep using it. The look of relief on her face had made it worth it. Besides, Yasmin liked to pretend she was fine with things when she was actually not. If she really needed the calculator and Mal took it back, Yasmin might resent her for it. And Mal hated the thought of anyone resenting her. Sure it took a lot longer to do her homework on the online calculator she found, but she'd catch up in math eventually.

"I saw you talking to Jaydon during class," K.K. said at their lunch table later, lifting her perfectly plucked eyebrows. K.K.'s short, natural hair was pulled back into a high puff today, the edges smoothed carefully into swoops. Mal brushed her own messy bangs out of her face and rolled her eyes.

"Like I told you a bajillion times," Mal said, opening her lunch bag. "I don't like him anymore. He was just borrowing a pencil."

"Did you know bajillion isn't a real number?" Wendy said, peeling her clementine. "Neither are zillion or gazillion."

"You're just trying to change the subject," K.K. said, grinning at Wendy. "Because you and Jaydon were talking for*ever* after math. Are you a thing now?"

Wendy made a choking sound and reached for her water.

"Ohhhh, I see," Mal said playfully. "So that's who he likes. I knew it wasn't me."

"It's nothing!" Wendy said, wiping her mouth. "He was just asking about my science project." She looked up at a table full of skeptical faces. "Well, it's true," she said.

"You like him. And he likes you," Etta declared matter-of-factly, plopping down across from them. "We all know it."

"He seems super sweet," Mal said.

"And he's cute," said K.K. "That new fade of his . . ." She made a chef's kiss motion with her fingers and kissed at the air.

Wendy became very interested in picking every tiny bit of white off her wedges of clementine. Her ears were bright red.

"So, how far are you in *Battlestar*?" Mal asked Wendy, stabbing a nugget with her fork. "You know," she added, raising her voice dramatically, "the nerdy sci-fi show I got you into?"

K.K. laughed and stood with a wave of her hand. "Okay, nerds, I get the hint," she said as she left the table. "I have student council things to do anyway."

Wendy gave Mal a relieved look, and Mal grinned. She was good at reading Wendy, and right now Wendy needed to talk *Battlestar Galactica*.

"How much do you love Starbuck?" Mal asked her. "I still can't believe how she crawled inside that alien ship!"

"She's the only one that I'm one hundred percent sure is not secretly a Cylon at this point," Wendy said.

"A what?" Etta asked, shoveling Tater Tots into her mouth.

"Cylons are these evil alien robots," Mal explained. "But they look just like humans."

Etta wrinkled her pale, freckled nose. "Not really my thing, but I can see why you two would like it." She popped a whole baby carrot into her mouth.

"Why are you eating so fast?" Wendy asked her.

"GSA," Etta said around her mouthful of carrot. "We're

going to paint the new gender-neutral bathroom on the second floor after lunch."

"And you have permission this time?" Mal asked. Principal Whitman had almost lost her mind when she found Etta painting a whole mural in the hallway a couple of weeks ago. She'd done it only to cover up hateful graffiti targeting immigrant kids, particularly Latine kids like Wendy. Etta had turned the wall into a starry sky, since Wendy loved astronomy. Mal had helped Etta paint the words "You Belong" in giant bubble letters along the bottom, and it had turned into a communal project with kids adding their own messages of inclusion. But she still couldn't believe Etta had gotten away with it.

"It is fully authorized," Etta said. She pointed a carrot at Mal. "You should come with me."

Mal wasn't sure what to say. She took a bite of food instead.

Wendy looked surprised. "Are you part of the GSA?" she asked Mal. Mal shook her head no. She *had* thought about joining the Gay-Straight Alliance. But she wasn't entirely sure if the GSA was her thing.

"I'm . . . not queer," she told Etta. It came out like a question.

Etta shot her a dubious look, and Mal squirmed. She *had* told Etta all about that girl she met at her Korean camp. The girl with the great laugh who, one night around the campfire, had held Mal's hand.

"Well . . . ," Mal said. "I mean, I *might* have liked a girl this summer. Kind of. But I don't know." She picked at her food. It had definitely felt like a crush. But then she'd sort of fallen for Jaydon when school started. So maybe what happened at camp hadn't meant anything.

"Well," Etta continued, turning to Wendy now, "straight is actually in the name too. At least for now. Miss Hill says we're changing the name to 'Gender and Sexuality Alliance,' but either way, allies are welcome!" She crunched down on her last carrot.

Mal took another bite and didn't say anything. The GSA sounded like the kind of place where everyone had a name for themselves. Mal imagined glitter-covered name tags where everyone had to write down some kind of LGBTQIA+ term before they could enter. *Gay. Lesbian. Nonbinary. Trans.* So many labels. She had no idea what she would write on hers.

"You could start today if you want," Etta said. "Come help us paint when you finish eating, okay?"

Mal chewed slowly, trying to figure out what Etta wanted. Did she want Mal to say she was queer? Maybe the GSA just needed help painting? Mal could do that at least.

"Yeah, okay," Mal agreed.

Etta rewarded her with a giant grin as she popped out of her seat. Mal watched Etta's pink hair disappear into the lunch crowd. She hated saying no to things. Besides, it gave her a warm feeling to see her friends smile like that. Even if she didn't have a GSA name tag, her "good friend" label was solidly in place.

But when she left the cafeteria, Mal forgot all about Etta's paint project. A tall Black boy was posting a notice in the hallway, and he almost collided with Mal as he stepped away from the wall. He put up his hands, apologizing with an awkward smile. Mal started to reassure him that it was fine, but her eyes landed on the paper sign. Her words stuttered to a stop. Was that a robot? And a fierce-looking manga girl? The boy went on his way, but Mal stayed frozen in the middle of the hall, her checked Vans rooted to the floor. Hand-drawn manga and anime characters lined the bottom of the flyer. Mal pushed her glasses up her nose, squinting at the pictures. One of the sketches looked a lot like the cyborg hero from her webcomic. And that robot next to her could be one of Zee's crew.

There's no way someone from LPA drew my characters on a school flyer, Mal told herself. *Absolutely no way.*

Her eyes flew to the words in the center. *"Do you love comics? Join us at the Rooville library after school for COMIC CLUB! Mondays and Wednesdays!"*

Mal bit her lip. A comic club? She wondered if she could get out of watching her brothers after school. It might be fun to meet up with other kids who liked comics. More important, she needed to figure out who had made this flyer. And how much they knew about *Metal-Plated Heart*.

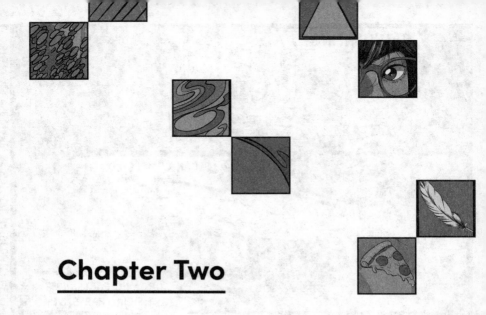

Chapter Two

SPLASH! **BROTH SPLATTERED OVER MALLORY'S** Doctor Who shirt. She stared down at the rubber bouncy ball in her bowl of ramen. It bobbed gently among the noodles, bits of greenish-brown vegetable flakes sticking to its red surface.

"Sorry!" Wyatt yelled. Mallory squinted at him through the blur of droplets dotting her glasses. She knew it was Wyatt because everything he said came out like he was using a bullhorn. "Winston threw it!" he yelled.

"Did not!" Winston yelled back from the other side of the room. "Liar!"

"Liar!" That was Wyatt again.

"Liar!" Winston yelled back.

The twins' voices melded in perfect unison, like paired speakers.

"Liar!"

"Liar!"

"Liar!"

Mallory took off her glasses and wiped them on the hem of her T-shirt. She carried her dishes to the kitchen, feeling an instant relief as she moved away from the surround sound of miniature fury. As Mal rinsed off the bouncy ball in the sink, she glanced at the clock. Ten minutes until Mom got home. In the next room her brothers' yelling devolved into a wrestling match. Mal took a fortifying breath before stepping back into the dining room.

"Who wants ice cream?" Mal called.

"Me!" The twins tumbled apart and raced toward her.

"Hang on," Mal said. "You know Mom's rule. Dishes first!"

Wyatt groaned but sped to the table to clear his bowl. Winston looked up at Mal, his dark eyes pleading. "Where's my ball, Mal-Mal?"

Mom would make him clear his bowl first. But there was a familiar whine creeping into Winston's voice. Mallory hated it when he whined.

"Promise to clear your bowl?" Mal asked.

Winston nodded eagerly. She handed him the ball. Anything to stop a tantrum.

Winston immediately threw the ball at the floor with all his kindergarten might. The ball bounced upward and rebounded off the ceiling just as Wyatt flew out of the kitchen, slamming into the ball and bouncing it into the living room.

"Hey!" Winston yelled.

They took off again and Mal closed her eyes. So much for Babysitting Rule #3: *Everyone do their chores. Well,* she told herself, *as long as they get done.* She cleared the rest of the dishes and grabbed the ice cream sandwiches from the freezer.

The twins crash-landed at the table and tore open the sandwiches.

"Wyatt, don't lick the table!" Mal said. "Just eat it before it melts."

Winston, his mouth already full of creamy vanilla, whispered loudly, "Stop, Wyatt! You're making Mal mad!"

"Mal-Mal never gets mad," Wyatt yelled, and took a huge bite.

Wyatt was right. Mal didn't get mad. But sometimes she could feel something simmering deep in her core. Writing down notes in her sketchbook helped keep that feeling in check. Mal looked at the twins' full, sticky mouths and reached for her sketchbook. *W&W: Full mouths = silence,* she wrote. Dubs, the two-headed alien cat that ran around creating chaos in her webcomic, was a fan favorite. But it might be nice for Zee if Dubs's mouths got stuck shut now and then.

"Please, Mal?" Wyatt's voice filtered through her thoughts. "Can you?"

"What?" she asked distractedly.

"Will you play too? In our room?"

Mal tapped her pencil, her mind on her webcomic. "Oh, um," she said, glancing up at her brother, "not right now. You guys play by yourselves, okay?"

Mal was sketching a scene where Zee plans an undercover heist when the front door opened. Mal gave herself a shake, bringing her attention back to reality. The boys were nowhere to be seen and her mom was coming in the door, a stack of files balanced in one arm as she slipped off her heels.

"Hi, Mom!" Mal said. "How was work?"

Her mom flashed a quick smile but lifted one finger to signal for Mal to wait. Her phone was pressed to her ear.

"Double-check the dates on that third document," she said in her work voice. Her neat black hair was still in the sleek bun from that morning. It perfectly matched her slim black peacoat and her gray pencil skirt. Mom always looked like she belonged in some kind of magazine with a title like "Power Women of Tomorrow." Mal watched her mom lean forward to set the files on the table, then freeze, her eyes taking in the spilled broth and smears of ice cream. Mal jumped up and grabbed the dishcloth. Her mom nodded a thanks and kept talking, setting the files down gracefully as soon as Mal had wiped a spot clean.

Mal watched her mom for a moment, feeling her own shoulders straighten as they always did around Magnolia Marsh. *Magnolia Jeong*, Mal corrected herself. Not Marsh anymore. It was still weird to think of her mom with her maiden name. She knew it shouldn't be weird. But Mallory and her brothers had always been Marshes. And so had Mom, until three months ago.

"We both know the paperwork won't be done in time," Mom was saying. Mal grabbed her sketchbook and headed upstairs. She might be able to get through another few panels before bedtime.

Crash!

It was the thick, destructive sound of breaking wood. Exactly the kind of sound you didn't want to hear from a kids' bedroom. Mal ran toward the boys' room but her mom got there first. She peeked around her mom to see a broken piece of the wooden bed board lying on the heap of clothes and toys under one of the boys' loft beds. Winston's horrified face hung upside down off the end of the bed.

"Oh my gods," Mal muttered.

"Mallory," her mom said in an exasperated tone.

"Sorry," Mal apologized quickly. Mom had grown up

attending Korean church, where words like "God" weren't used casually. Mom didn't really mind, and she even got a kick out of Mallory saying "oh my gods" or "oh my goddesses," but she didn't want the boys to pick up on it in case they repeated it around their halmoni.

The heap of clothes under the broken board moved. Her mom gasped and jumped forward, crouching down to lift the splintered pieces of wood. Wyatt looked up from the floor, the beginnings of a lump showing on his forehead just under his short black hair.

"Wyatt, sweetie, are you all right?" Mom asked.

Wyatt mumbled something.

Mal heard a whimper and looked up to see Winston's face crumple. Oh no. He was about to start wailing. Mal felt herself torn between wanting to comfort her brother and wanting to run away and bury her head under the blankets before it started. Before Mal could decide, Wyatt sat straight up and grinned. "Again!"

Mal stared at her brother. So did Mom.

"Young man, are you asking to do this"— Mom waved at the broken pieces of wood— "again?"

Wyatt nodded happily. "We were swinging!" He held up something fluffy and pastel blue. Mal recognized it as the belt to her mom's bathrobe. One end was tied to the broken bed board. He looked up at his mother, then his face changed as he registered her expression. His eyes grew wide and innocent. "Mal said we could!"

Mal's own eyebrows shot up in surprise as Mom turned her stern look on her. Wait, had she? She struggled to remember what had happened after the ice cream. Her brothers had asked her if she wanted to play. Had they asked if they could raid their mother's closet and make swings on their loft beds? She was sure that she wouldn't have agreed to that. But honestly, her mind had been pretty far away on E-1: the original Earth, and the fight against the oppressive Disposal Authority.

"I'm so sorry. We had a minor household accident." Mom's work voice interrupted her thoughts. "Yes, I'd better go now. Take care." Mom ended the call and slid her phone into the pocket of the peacoat she was still wearing. Even crouched on the floor she managed to look professional.

"Mom, I'm sorry," Mal started to say. "I didn't say they could—"

Just then, Winston began to wail. Mallory cringed. If Wyatt spoke like a bullhorn, Winston wailed like a fire alarm.

"Mallory," Mom said, raising her voice over the noise as she stood up and reached toward the loft bed for Winston. "Please start the dishwasher while I get your brothers ready for bed." Mal felt the punch of Mom's disappointment hit her deep in the gut. "And then homework," Mom added. "I'll be up in about an hour to check in."

When the house had finally settled into the quiet that came only with sleeping twins, Mom came into Mal's room for her usual nightly check-in. Mal was on her bed, with her assigned reading book in hand and *One Piece* streaming on her laptop.

"Screens off, my dear," Mom said. She looked tired. No surprise after dealing with the boys. Mal snapped the laptop shut. Again, she tried to apologize.

"Mom, I really am—"

"Mallory, I know it's not your fault." Mom smiled at her, sitting on the edge of the bed. "They are a lot."

Mal nodded emphatically at that. "Wyatt's okay, though?"

"Oh yes. That kid is mostly rubber." Mom patted her arm reassuringly. "Are you done with homework? What are you reading?" She leaned closer.

"*Ghost*. It's Jason Reynolds. For ELA."

"Do you have much else to do?"

"Not really. Just some math."

Mom nodded, her eyes somewhere else. Mal could practically see her mom's brain running through her nightly To-Do list. *Tuck in boys—check. Ask Mal about homework— check.*

"I am sorry about all the extra hours, Mal-Mal," Mom said, her eyes coming back to Mallory's. "There's just been so much with the new cases I've taken on."

"Oh, I know. It's okay. It's just for one more week. I can

handle it. And I'll make sure they don't turn their beds into a trapeze again." Mal smiled, hoping to look confident.

But Mom didn't smile back. "Well," she said carefully. "It's actually going to be a bit longer than that."

Mal waited, keeping her face neutral and pleasant.

"I've been asked to take on a more permanent role," Mom said. "It will be a lot of hours, but the truth is . . ." She sighed. "I can't say no. Not right now."

Mom was a paralegal, and she had started taking on extra projects at the law firm last spring. At the time it hadn't changed things too much at home. But that was before Dad moved out. He and Mom had been talking about it for nearly a year, so the separation wasn't exactly a shock. But with Dad paying for a new apartment and with the divorce fees and paperwork . . . Well, Mal paid attention. It didn't surprise her that Mom needed the extra money. But it still gave her a dull ache in her belly to think of Mom always coming home so late.

"So I will need you to keep on watching the boys."

Mal's brain flashed for just a moment to the flyer on the wall at school. *Comic club. Mondays and Wednesdays after school.* She had hoped that maybe . . . But she looked at her mom and let a smile ease onto her face. A professional, purposeful smile, like Mom's. She knew what Mom needed right now.

"No problem."

Her mom patted her arm again.

24

"That's my responsible girl." Mom leaned forward like she had something special to share. "And guess what?"

"What?" Mal asked.

"I saw Coach Perkins today. Pure happenstance. We were at the same café downtown. And I realized I had completely forgotten about swim team!" Mom gave a little laugh of disbelief.

Mal felt her stomach sink.

"We've had so much going on that we almost missed it completely!" Mom said, shaking her head.

"I think we did miss it," Mal said. "I'm sure the deadline to register must have passed already." It had. Mal knew exactly when the deadline had been—last Wednesday. She had waited all day for her mom to say something. When bedtime arrived with no mention of registering, Mal had sighed in relief and slept with the peace of a deactivated robot. Now she gave a disappointed shrug. "It's too late."

Mom's smile positively twinkled. "Well, it would be, if your mother weren't such a good persuader! I convinced Coach Perkins to sign you up right away. Of course, we still had to pay the full amount plus a late registration fee." Her smile faltered, and Mal could almost see the financial calculations happening in her mom's brain.

"Oh, Mom, no, please don't pay for that," Mal said quickly. "I really don't have to do it and we need the money for other—"

Mom held up a hand to stop her. "No, Mal-Mal. This is important to you. Besides, I've already paid. No refunds. They started practice Monday, so you've missed four days. But he said you can start tomorrow!" She beamed at Mal.

Mallory swallowed hard, her throat tight. "Wow."

"I've arranged for the boys to have after-school care at the community center until five. You can drop them off after school, then swim to your heart's content. After practice, you just pick them up and walk home." Mom sighed in satisfaction. "We are truly fortunate to live in a neighborhood like Rooville with so many resources in walking distance."

Mal nodded mechanically. Her mom had everything figured out. All the loose ends were tied up and tucked in, smooth and neat just like her hair bun.

"Mom—" Mal started to say.

"Mal, listen. I want you to know how truly sorry I am for all that I've had to ask of you lately." Mom reached out and tucked a strand of messy hair behind Mal's ear. "I'm just so glad we could at least make this work for you. I know how much you love to swim."

"I'm just not sure I should do swim team this year," Mal said. The words came out small and tight, like they had been squeezed from a tube.

Mom's expression changed and Mal hurried to add, "It's not that I don't *want* to. But it's extra money and time and it's so intense sometimes. . . ." She trailed off.

Mom voice had a stern edge to it now as she said, "Mallory Marsh. Do you remember what it was like when you hurt your ankle last year and had to stop swimming for the rest of the season?"

Mal looked down. She had a feeling she knew where this was going.

"You spent all your time shut up in your room." Mal could hear the disapproval in Mom's voice. "I won't have you sitting at home after school every day, wasting time doodling and staring at screens."

Mal opened her mouth to say her comics were more than just doodles. But Mom shot her a look. Mal gulped. Mom didn't know that Mal spent most of her screen time on Comic Koala. She *couldn't* know that. Or she'd shut down *Metal-Plated Heart* for good. "You're completely right, Mom," she said.

Mom looked at her, narrowing her eyes. Mal forced the tension out of her face and smiled at her. "I *do* want to swim, Mom. Thanks for making it all work out."

Mom's face softened, and Mal saw a look in her eyes that reminded her of Winston when he asked for his ball. Something small and pleading. "It really does work perfectly, doesn't it?"

"Yep," Mal agreed. "It's perfect, Mom."

Mom gave her a pleased smile.

"Jal ja, Mal-Mal," Mom said. Her lips touched Mal's

forehead and then Mom was gone. *Ruin Mal's life—check.*

Mal lay back against her pillow, letting *Ghost* fall shut with a thud. She did love to swim. But turning it into an organized sport ruined everything. When she joined the swim team two years ago, it hadn't really mattered that she wasn't competitive. Her old coach was a peace-loving hippie who had started and ended each practice with deep breathing and mindfulness exercises. But at the end of last year, the rec center had hired Coach Perkins, who had been on the swim team in college. Mal only survived the season because her ankle injury kept her out for most of the meets. If she had to go through a full season with him, she would just implode one day underwater, like a punctured soccer ball. She would drift to the bottom and never come up. And if she was spending every afternoon at swim, every evening watching the boys, and every night doing her homework, when would she work on *Metal-Plated Heart?*

Chapter Three

WHEN MAL SLID HER SKETCHBOOK INTO HER backpack the next morning, it caught on her swim towel. She frowned as she shoved the towel down and zipped her bag carefully closed. It was the same backpack she'd gotten in fifth grade, and it was barely holding together. Today she'd stuffed all her swim things into her bag, plus the boys' after-school snacks, her binder, her copy of *Ghost*, and her book for social studies. Then there was her usual stuff—Chromebook, keys, wallet, her zippered pouch of period supplies, first aid kit, phone, eco-friendly water bottle covered in decals, and her TARDIS pencil case. Mallory liked to be prepared.

As she waited with her brothers to cross Main and Willow, Mal heard a whimper. She looked down at Winston.

"Mal-Mal," her brother said. He sounded close to tears. "Is the kitty lost?"

Mal followed his gaze. A printed sign stapled to a corner post read, "Lost Cat." There was a picture of a fluffy white cat with caramel patches sitting in a box. Underneath the picture it read: "Fluffernutter. Friendly, adored, and very missed."

"What's that for?" Winston asked, pointing to the row of paper flaps along the bottom with the phone number printed on each.

"It's so people can take the phone number with them," Mal explained, looking at the crosswalk sign. "So they know who to call if they find the cat."

Just as the light changed, Wyatt grabbed for a paper flap and pulled so hard that a large corner of the page ripped off. "Oops!" he yelled.

Winston stared at the strip of paper flaps in his brother's hand. There was only one left hanging on the poster. "Wyatt!" he said, sounding horrified. "Now people won't know who to call!"

Mal looked from the crossing light to Winston's wide, worried eyes and the ripped poster. She groaned. Mal set down her backpack and dug for the roll of tape she always carried. The twins held the ripped paper in place while she taped it carefully back together. They had to wait for the next crossing signal, but the relief on Winston's face was worth it. *Thank you, backpack*, Mal thought. *Kindergarten meltdown avoided.*

At school that day, Mal gave out three pencils, loaned out her copy of *Ghost*, and handed someone a granola bar when she overheard that they'd skipped breakfast. She complimented a girl who had just gotten glasses and joked around with a kid who needed cheering up. After lunch, K.K. pulled her along to reapply their makeup in the bathroom. K.K's mom was a cosmetologist and K.K. had grown up in the salon. She'd quickly become the resident seventh-grade makeup expert at LPA, especially on products for non-white skin. Mal had said something about Korean beauty products once and K.K. had immediately assumed Mal was just as into makeup as she was. Mal didn't correct her, even though the feeling of smearing foundation on her skin made her shiver inside. But K.K. loved having someone to share her beauty routines with, so Mal went along with it. Every time Mal saw someone's face light up as she handed them exactly what they needed or when she said just the right thing, she knew she was doing it right. She was who she was supposed to be.

But as swim practice drew closer, Mal felt more and more on edge. How was she supposed to get through a whole season of Coach Perkins shouting, "I said streamline, Marsh! You'll never beat anyone with that speed, Marsh!" By the time she picked up the boys from their elementary school, Mallory had a plan. She dropped off the twins at the aftercare room in the community center and then raced down the hall to the pool office. She swiped her card under the scanner to sign in, then stepped up to the desk. "A set of earplugs, please," she told the teen folding towels into neat stacks.

Mal didn't usually swim with earplugs, but today she pressed them in with a feeling of immense gratitude. The usual underwater noises of a busy pool were completely muffled. Mal relaxed as all thoughts of who she was supposed to be melted away. In the pool, it didn't matter that Mal wasn't skinny or athletic. Her muscles felt like a gift, strong enough to push her through the space around her. She was nearly done with her last lap when her brain registered a distant roaring sound. It was getting louder. She slowed, treading water and lifting her head toward the roar. The dark blur of Coach Perkins loomed at the edge of the pool, his voice dulled by the earplugs.

"—should be on backstroke now. Your stroke hasn't changed for five laps! I told you—" Coach Perkins cut off, his brown cheeks flushing. "Are you wearing earplugs, Marsh? How do you expect to hear instructions if you wear earplugs?"

Oh no.

Mal hauled herself out of the pool as Coach Perkins shouted at her to take them out. She walked toward the bench as Coach Perkins yelled at another kid to keep his toes pointed. Everything he said sounded angry, even the "good job, Mulligan!" he called out as Fiona did a quick flip turn. Mal set her earplugs down on her towel with a sinking heart.

Without the earplugs, Mal could feel her inner peace leaking away. The sound around her built like waves, hammering into her consciousness. Coach stopped her three times during her next lap. Her kicks were weak, her head wasn't angled right, her strokes still weren't high enough. Mal wanted to curl into a ball and let herself fall like a rock to the bottom of the pool.

When practice finally ended, Mal dragged her body from the locker room and toward the exit.

"It'll get easier, Marsh!" Coach shouted after her. "See you Monday, same time!"

Mal stopped. Panic swelled in her gut. Monday. She had to do all of this again next week.

"I can't," she blurted.

He frowned. "Why's that?"

"Because," she said, swallowing, "Mondays I have . . ." Her brain raced. Then, like a beam of light, it hit her. "Comic club. It's like a book club. At the library. On Mondays. And Wednesdays."

For a moment, Coach just stared down at her, his eyebrows drawn together like one black, furry caterpillar. Then he grunted and shouted in an almost-normal speaking voice, "Literacy is important, Marsh! Have your mom message me about your new schedule. See you Tuesday!"

Mal felt her whole body sag with relief as he turned back to the pool. She had managed to get out of swim for two afternoons. And with her brothers in aftercare, she could even check out comic club. But what would Mom say?

She worried about what Mom would say through the long, noisy walk home with her brothers. She worried during the long, noisy dinner with the pizza she had picked up on their way home (double pepperoni, their usual). And she worried during the long, noisy evening of trying to keep them happy and in one piece. When Mom finally got home, Mal watched her carefully, waiting for the right moment to bring it up.

But with the twins around there were no right moments. A firefighter had visited their kindergarten class that morning and now Winston wanted a thorough fire safety home review. He followed Mom from room to room as she pointed out the smoke detectors.

"Let's practice escaping!" Wyatt yelled. He ran through Mom's bedroom to the window.

Winston called after him, "No, Wyatt! We have to *crawl* to the window!" He threw himself to the floor and crawled after his brother.

Mom moaned and pressed her fingertips to her forehead. "No windows!" she called, hurrying after Wyatt.

Maybe I'll talk to her at bedtime, Mal thought, heading to her room. She needed to do her math homework anyway.

But instead she found herself logging on to Comic Koala. The iconic koala illustration greeted her, tough and adorable in its mech armor. The sight filled her with a soft, bubbly happiness. Comic Koala was Mal's go-to comfort site. And it was based at the brick-and-mortar comic shop just a few blocks away, right here in Columbus, Ohio. The real-life Comic Koala was one of Mal's favorite places in the whole world. The shop was made up of three old brick houses that had been joined together. It was full of passages and narrow stairways leading to a seemingly endless maze of rooms. Each room burst with bookshelves full of comics and books. Part of the house was blocked off and Mal was pretty sure the owner, S.J. Summerhill, lived there. She'd never met her, but she knew her from her online posts and comics.

A new comment notification pinged in the corner of her screen. It was a comment on "Episode 10: Top of the Charts," the one that had the most views. Not too surprising. Mal clicked on the comment.

Great writing and message on this epi. Well done, Dr.BotGirl. We need more creators willing to stand up to hate. You've got a fan in me. I look forward to your next one.

Mal stopped breathing. The comment was from S.J.theBoss. The moderator of Comic Koala. The published author with at least five print comic books and several online serials. S.J. Summerhill.

Mal completely forgot how tired and stressed she had

felt a moment ago. Now she was vibrating with energy. S.J. Summerhill was looking forward to her next episode. This was better than all the upvotes she'd ever gotten. Mal could take pics of her completed panels tonight and start tracing them on her iPad. With any luck she'd have something new up this weekend. Mal dived into her sketchbook, all thoughts of math homework or talking to Mom far from her mind.

Chapter Four

AT LUNCH ON MONDAY, MAL'S USUAL TABLE WAS empty. K.K., who was vice president of their junior high, had a student council meeting. Yasmin always ate in the library so she'd have time for her midday prayer. Wendy, whose winning science fair project was going on to the district competition, was working with Ms. Park during lunch. The GSA was still painting the gender-neutral bathroom. Etta didn't even sit down; she just scarfed down a blueberry muffin as soon as she left the food line.

"You wanna come?" Etta said, popping the last bit of muffin in her mouth. She bounced on her toes, full of energy.

"I think we're almost done! I'm just filling in the giant rainbow today. And Miss Hill said she'd give us all rainbow flag pins as a thank-you."

Mal grinned back at her, feeling herself mirroring Etta's excitement. Mal held up her full tray. "I totally would but I don't eat as fast as you."

"It's okay," Etta said, walking backward toward the door. "If there are extra pins I'll bring you one." She held up one finger, like she was about to make an important point. "But *only* if you want it." She grinned mischievously, like they were sharing a secret.

"Oh yeah, definitely," Mal said, giving her a matching smile. "I'll take one if there's an extra."

"Great!" Etta said, still walking backward. "You don't have to wear it yet, you know." Then Etta ran into a kid behind her and nearly made him drop his tray. She apologized, stood his juice box back up on his tray, waved to Mal, and skipped away. She was the only person Mal knew who actually, literally skipped.

As she slid into a seat across from Fiona, a girl from swim, it hit Mal what Etta must have meant. *You don't have to wear it yet*, she had said. *Oh*, Mal thought, an uncomfortable feeling prickling the back of her neck. Etta totally thought Mal was a lesbian but not ready to come out yet. She thought about that secretive smile Etta had given her when she asked if she wanted a pride flag pin. Mal had smiled back and said

40

yes. . . . *She probably thought I was agreeing with her in some kind of . . . secret gay code? Was I? Or am I? Or—*

"So, Mallory," Fiona said, drawing out her name in a friendly, teasing way. "Whatcha thinking about?"

Mal had been staring off into space, munching on a bite of cafeteria pizza. "Oh," she said, "sorry, nothing."

"*We* think," said a girl named Sabrina, "that you're thinking about a boy." She looked at Fiona and giggled.

For a second Mal felt like her insides were being stretched out like bubble gum: Etta on one side, pulling her toward the GSA, and these girls on the other, whispering about boys. Still, she looked at their excited faces and felt like they were inviting her in. There was something nice about her friends sharing something special with her, even if it was totally off base.

"You got me!" she said, giggling along with Fiona and trying to look embarrassed.

Fiona gave a little squeal. "I knew it! Who is it, Mal? Tell, tell, tell!"

Mal shook her head no, waving a finger back and forth at Fiona. She didn't have a name to tell them anyway. She'd crushed hard on Jaydon at the beginning of the year, after he forgot his lunch and Mal gave him hers. Maybe it had something to do with the way he looked at her when she'd offered it to him, like a supernatural sunbeam was shining down right on Mallory. But then she'd found out he liked someone else. It was easier to stay away from crushes altogether anyway.

"No fair," Fiona teased. "Tell us!"

Mal pretended to zip her lips shut.

"Okay," Sabs said, nodding at Mal. "We respect the zip."

"I don't care who it is as long as it's not Brett," Fiona said.

Mal looked at her in surprise. "I thought you broke up?" she said.

"We did," Fiona said, tossing her wavy blond hair. She put a hand on Mal's shoulder. "Mallory, you are a decent human being, and I would not wish Brett Cobb on my worst enemy." She lowered her voice dramatically and whispered, "Save yourself!"

Mal grinned. "Oh, he's got no chance with me. Unless he totally replaces his personality."

Sabrina nodded. "He is awful."

"You know what else is awful? This piece of cardboard garbage," Fiona said, curling her lip at the limp square of cafeteria pizza.

"Yeah, this pizza is nasty," Mal agreed. She poked her fork at the rubbery layer of cheese.

"Pizza days in here just make me crave Pizza Pundit," Sabs said.

Fiona squealed. "I *love* Pizza Pundit!"

Pizza Pundit was the absolute best food spot in their neighborhood. Maybe in the whole city, actually. It was cheap and greasy and amazing. Every pizza was named after a pundit—some media person who was famous for talking about politics or movies or something. Their mini pizzas were the perfect size for two or three kids to split and it was only one block from school, so it was a favorite after-school hangout.

"Oh my gods, yes," Mal said. "I just had some last night."

"Which one?" Fiona asked. "I'd kill for a slice of The Jake right now instead of this. It is hands down the best pizza ever. I don't care that it's just cheese because It. Is. Perfection."

"The Jake is my fave," Sabrina agreed.

Mal nodded. "Yeah, me too. The Jake is great." The Jake was fine, if a little plain. Mal's family usually ordered The Van because her brothers loved double pepperoni. It didn't matter to Mal. All the choices at Pizza Pundit were delicious.

"Ooooooh, we should go after school!" Sabs said.

"No way," Fiona said. "Not right before swimming, right, Mal?"

"Right," Mal said, her heart sinking as she remembered the lie she'd told Coach Perkins. "Actually, Fiona, I'm not—"

"Hey!" Fiona tipped her head to one side, peering around Sabs. "Speaking of swim, there are those guys from the team! You know, Mal, those two who are, like, cousins or something? They have those dark eyes and those muscles?" She giggled.

Sabs started to turn, but Fiona grabbed her hand and

pulled. "No! The cute one is looking!"

Mal let her eyes roam casually over to the table where the boys were sitting. *Oh, them.* She *had* noticed them at swim. Fiona was right about the muscles.

"What are you talking about?" Mal whispered out of the side of her mouth. "They are *both* super cute!"

Sabs looked like not turning around was physically painful. *"Who?"*

Fiona was still giggling. "Hang on! Cutie is seriously looking right this way. Okay, Cutie number one. They *are* both cute but number two has, like, a crooked nose or something."

"But that's why he's cute," Mal said. "He's interesting. Don't you want him to tell you how he broke his nose rescuing a kitten from in front of a speeding car or something?"

Fiona pretended to think about it for half a second. "Nope! I'd rather just stare into number one's dreamy, dark eyes—"

"While you stroke his perfectly straight nose?" Mal asked, trailing her fingers dramatically through the air. Fiona snorted and they both dissolved into giggles.

Sabs groaned. "This is not fair." She pulled away from Fiona and twisted around.

Fiona squealed and ducked behind Mal.

"Ooooooh! Why did I not join swim team?" Sabs said, staring openly at the boys.

"Fiona, I think he saw you looking!" Mal teased.

Fiona gasped and clutched at the back of Mal's denim jacket. Sabs turned back, laughing. "She's just messing with you, Fee. They are not paying any attention. But seriously, you two are so lucky."

Fiona sat back up, giggling. "This swim season is going to *rule*!" she said, throwing an arm around Mallory. Mal made herself smile and nod in agreement, even though her stomach was twisting at the thought. "Go, Rooville Rapids!" she said, squeezing Fiona back.

Mal had spent all weekend perfecting and posting her latest episode, so she hadn't had a chance to ask about comic club. When Mom reminded her to take her swim stuff that morning, Mal just shoved it in her bag. It was easier to let Mom think she was going to practice. Now she stood outside the community center, digging under her towel for the boys' snacks.

"Can I come to swimming?" Winston asked.

"What? Why?" Mal asked. "And where's Wyatt?" she added, looking around.

Wyatt had stopped at the Branch Tree. Of all the trees in the courtyard, this one was the best. Its lowest branch swooped down and then back up like an invitation. The curve of its bark was worn smooth from all the older kids who had climbed it, even though they weren't supposed to. The twins always called it "the Branch Tree," and they dreamed of one day being tall enough to jump up, grab ahold, and pull themselves onto that perfect branch.

"Wyatt, come on! I have chocolate chip!"

Wyatt gave a useless jump toward the branch and then ran over. Mal handed him a granola bar.

"So, can I? Pleeeeease?" Winston pleaded through a mouthful.

"No," Mal said, herding the boys toward the doors. "Why would you want to come watch other people swim anyway?"

"The diving board is sooooo high," Winston said earnestly, his eyes wide. "Is it scary?"

"I'm just doing the swim team," Mal told him. "I don't dive."

"They don't let you," Winston said, nodding understandingly. "Maybe when you're bigger. Maybe if you swim good enough."

"It's not like that—" Mal started to say, but Wyatt yelled, "I can! I did one time! On the diving board up high! Like this!"

He jumped onto one of the park benches and put his hands out in front of him like Superman.

"Do *not* dive onto the sidewalk," Mal said, pulling him down. "Hey, race you!"

They arrived at the aftercare room in a stampede of running feet and gasping breaths. Mal signed her brothers in and walked down the hall. But instead of continuing to the pool, she went back out the door onto the sidewalk.

The air in the courtyard was crisp with an almost-winter chill, and Mallory breathed in deep. The afternoon sunlight shone through the mostly bare tree branches and she felt the tightness inside her unravel in the golden light. Across the courtyard stood the library, with its row of windows full of books. Where kids met to talk about comics. And where someone knew about *Metal-Plated Heart*. A twinge of worry soured the sunshine.

Suddenly, something caught Mal's eye. On the sidewalk across the courtyard stood a wheeled rack of clothes. And not just any clothes. They shimmered, actually shimmered, in a rainbow of different shades and fabrics. The riot of color stood out from the dull November brown around it like a portal to another dimension. She pushed her glasses up her nose and looked around. Who had left a rack of clothes in the middle of the sidewalk?

Mal shifted the straps of her backpack and walked over. Close-up, they were even more spectacular. The sunlight glinted on sequins in scarlet and sapphire. Tufts of butterscotch and tangerine tulle stuck out from the hanging fabric and a blue feather boa was looped over the top pole.

Just then there was a burst of noise as a crowd of aftercare kids raced out of the community center and onto the playground. Mal froze, her eyes immediately landing on Wyatt. He was at the front, racing to the swings, his sole focus obviously on getting there first. But Winston, his little face scrunched in concentration, was walking slowly away from the other kids, his eyes on something he held in both hands. He walked all the way up to the fence that separated the playground from the courtyard and stopped, still looking down.

Mal ducked behind the rack of clothes. Winston was a worrier. If he saw her hanging out in the courtyard instead of at the pool, Winston would worry. And when Winston worried, he went to Mom. She poked her hands between a sequined gown and a faux-fur shawl and pushed them apart enough to peek through. Her brother placed something tiny on one of the chain links in the fence. Probably a bug. He had a thing for bugs. She pushed the hangers back together again, letting her fingers glide over the fur and the sequins.

"You should go with the fur," said a voice behind her.

Mal whirled around.

Chapter Five

A BOX WITH A TOWER OF HATS HOVERED IN FRONT of her. All Mal could see of the kid holding it were light brown hands with purple fingernails gripping the bottom of the box. The hats were all fancy—the kind with beads and veils dotted with tiny pearls. A fountain of white feathers fanned up from one of them, hiding the bottom half of the person's face, and a lace-trimmed hat covered their head. They blew a puff of air at the lace and it fluttered. Behind it, Mal saw a flash of intense eyes rimmed with black eyeliner.

"Your dark hair would look amazing trailing down your

shoulders onto that white fur. Like a snow goddess!" Their voice was interesting, slightly musical but with a little rasp to it.

"Thanks," Mal said, blushing. She had never been called a snow goddess.

"Put it on!" They bounced up and down a bit as they spoke, like Etta might have done. Mal grinned because the voice seemed like it was grinning and the sound made her want to match that level of happy excitement. She looked back at the faux fur.

"Are these yours?" she asked.

"Well. Sort of." The box of hats jiggled and the feathers shifted to the side, revealing a kid Mal's age. They had a warm, brown-skinned face and an infectious smile. Ringlets of glossy deep brown hair peeked from under the lacy hat. Their eyes were a startling grayish-blue color. Mal felt a jolt in her belly, like static electricity. She wanted to step closer and look away at the same time.

"I should explain," said the person with the remarkable eyes. "Well, I should introduce myself first, I guess. Actually, hang on."

They crouched down, setting the box of hats on the sidewalk and standing back up. Their wool coat hung unbuttoned and under it they were wearing a pink-and-lavender plaid button-up shirt, tucked neatly into lavender pants. One pink feather earring dangled from their left ear. She hadn't seen this kid at school before. Their style was pretty unique, and they would stand out at LPA. And she had never made eye contact with them before, she was sure of that. She would have remembered that electric jolt.

"I'm Noa," the kid said, smiling. "But it's Noa with no H. That's too boy-y."

"Boy-y?" Mal asked.

"Yeah, you know. Standard masculine boy. Stupid, really. Tack on one H and suddenly everyone thinks I'm a boy. But I'm not. So it's N-o-a."

"Gotcha," Mal said. "No-boy Noa."

"No girl either, just to be clear. I'm just me. Noa. They/them pronouns. And yeah." They motioned to the rack of clothes. "These are temporarily mine. Mom was pushing it, but she got this far and my little sib threw a whale of a tantrum." Noa looked back toward the parking lot and waved merrily at a gray minivan with a dent on the side. The passenger window lowered and Mal heard the wail from inside. "Nap time," Noa said in explanation.

A frazzled-looking woman leaned out the window. She had the same rich brown curls and warm brown skin as Noa.

"It's okay!" Noa called. "I found help!" They looked at Mal. "You'll help me, right? I just need to get it to the library."

"Oh," Mal said, "yeah." She glanced toward the playground. Winston was looking in the direction of the crying toddler. "Of course!" She took hold of the rack, keeping it between her and Winston.

"Great!" Noa beamed at her and picked up the box. "What's your name?"

"Oh, I'm Mal," she answered. "Girl Mal. She/her. And I'll help you on one condition."

Noa's head tilted to the side, their feather earring swinging. Mal grinned at them. "I get to wear this one." She scooped the feathery hat from the top of the pile and plopped it on her head. Noa laughed.

"Only if you wear it with the fur," they said.

Perfect, Mal thought. *No way Winston will recognize me in this stuff.*

"Gorgeous!" Noa said as Mal pulled the shawl over her backpack. "That white feather and fur next to your dark hair—so dramatic. You belong on the stage."

Mal ducked her head. Her eyes flitted to Noa's again and she had to look away. Her heart actually sped up.

"Where did you get all this stuff anyway?" Mal asked as they headed down the sidewalk.

"Rick at the theater let me borrow it."

"The Rooville Theater?" Mal asked.

"Yep!" Noa grinned even wider and said in a confidential tone, "I'm in *all* the plays. Rick *loves* me. My Annie is legend."

"Really?" Mal said. "I'd like to see that."

"Well, *Annie* was last year. This year we did *The Secret Garden*. But it just finished."

"Were you Mary?" Mal asked. She couldn't picture Noa as

the grumpy, contrary little girl from *The Secret Garden*.

"Nope!" they said. "Dickon! You know, the boy from the moors? Talks to the animals and has eyes 'like a moorland sky.'" Noa said the last bit in a sort of British accent, batting their dark eyelashes. Mal wasn't sure what a "moorland sky" looked like, but if it was a misty, grayish-blue lined with black, then, yes, their eyes fit the description. Mal felt her stomach do a squirmy little flip. She looked back at the sidewalk, concentrating on guiding the wheeled rack over the cracks.

"So, are you doing a play with all this?"

"It's for Read with a Queen," Noa explained. "At the library. It's Reading Buddies but with a drag queen!"

"Wow," Mal said, not sure what else to say. She didn't know much about drag queens. "Like that one reality show?" Mal asked.

"*RuPaul's Drag Race*?" Noa asked, their eyes lighting up.

"Yeah. With the guys that dress up as women."

"I mean, that's the basic idea," Noa said. "But drag is *so* much more! It's a whole culture, a lifestyle, a . . ." They looked off into the distance. "A vibe." They grinned at Mal.

"So . . . the library is doing a program about drag queens?"

"No," Noa said earnestly. "A program *by* drag queens! There's this one drag queen, Shuga Toast, who does family-friendly shows. I saw her at the Pride parade last year, and it was so fun. She reads to kids during Reading Buddies, and it's a super inclusive, fun thing. They want to do it once a month."

"So this stuff is all for . . . her?" Mal wasn't sure if she was supposed to use female pronouns for a drag queen or not, but Noa had said *she* so it seemed like a safe guess.

"This stuff? Oh, no way! She has her own *fab*ulous wardrobe. I brought this for us!" Noa beamed at Mal and spun around toward the library doors.

"Um," Mal said, trying not to look as startled as she felt. "Us?" She pushed the clothes rack after Noa, wondering who they meant by *us*.

"Yep! And we're just in time," Noa called over their shoulder. "Come on!"

Mallory shot a quick glance across the courtyard at Winston. But he was crouched down on the ground, all his focus on something near his toes. She breathed a sigh of relief and pushed the rack into the warmth of the library.

Noa walked straight into the kids' area, dropped the box on a bright yellow chair, and threw out their arms. "I'm back, beautiful people!"

Mal followed them uncertainly, pushing the rack into the middle of the space. There were a couple of kids at computers who didn't even look up from their screens, but most of the kids moved toward the clothes like magnets. Lucy, the young Black woman who ran the Reading Buddies program, looked up from her sign-in sheet and gave a delighted wave.

"Noa! Wow, you weren't kidding when you said you were bringing Broadway to us!" She hurried to join the crowd of kids, her pencil earrings swinging. "These are incredible."

Noa doffed their hat, swinging it across their body and giving a deep bow. "At your service, milady!" Noa's hair was short in the back and on one side, but a pile of curls fell in an asymmetrical waterfall over their forehead. Noa tossed the floppy hat back in the box.

"Where should I put this?" they asked Lucy. "Rick said he doesn't want everyone playing with them." Noa looked at the kids' eager faces and grimaced. "Guess I should have thought of that before making an entrance," they said in a stage whisper.

Lucy laughed good-naturedly and told the kids the clothes were not for them. But they were already begging to try them on.

"Can I wear that one?"

"I want the sparkle tutu!

"Ooooooh," said one little boy, running his hands over the red sequined dress. "Pitty."

Lucy crouched down to his level and said, "Let's use our eyes, not our hands, okay? These are very special costumes."

Noa shot an abashed look back at Mal. "I gotta work on my subtlety," they said.

"Noa, there is not a subtle bone in your whole body," said a Black girl about their age. She crossed her arms over her baggy sweater vest. "You literally announced your entrance to the entire library."

"Only because I knew you were all desperately awaiting my arrival," Noa said, wiggling their eyebrows mischievously. "Oh, Izzy, this is Mal. She helped me bring this in."

Mal gave the girl a small wave.

"You're conscripting innocent bystanders again?" Izzy said. She gave Mal an apologetic look. "So sorry. Once they've got you locked in, you can't get out. It's like a Noa tractor beam, pulling you in."

"Izzy, tell me you did not just compare me to the Death Star," Noa said in a horrified voice.

"Hey, you're a force. You can use it for good. You don't *have* to destroy entire planets."

A little kid sneezed loudly, wiped his face, then reached for a lacy hat. Noa scooped up the box just in time and held it out of reach. They shot Mal a desperate look and mouthed, "*Help!*"

"Lucy," Mal said. "Do you want us to put these in the back?"

"Oh my goodness! Is that Mallory Marsh?" Lucy said, peering at her. "I didn't even recognize you in that hat! Yes, the back is great." She waved them over to the staff door and swiped her badge. "Go ahead and put it all in my office," Lucy told them. "And if you want to pick out what you're wearing, you can head straight to the meeting room. Shuga

Toast is already in there!"

What you're wearing? Mal thought, looking at the rack of clothes. She had the strangest sense that she was slipping on a patch of ice at the top of a cliff. Why did it sound like she was about to do some kind of performance?

"Um, Noa?" she said, but Noa was already heading through the door with the box. Izzy held it open for Mal to follow. Noa cheerily greeted the staff in the back room and they waved, greeting Noa, Izzy, and Mallory by name.

Mal stammered hello and pushed the rack to Lucy's office.

"Everyone knows you two here, don't they?" Mal asked them.

"Well, I *am* rather memorable." Noa grinned, taking off their coat and tossing it over a chair. "Izzy and I are both in comic club. And today our club is helping with Reading Buddies."

Comic club, Mal thought, looking at them both. Maybe one of them had made that flyer? Did one of them know about her webcomic?

"Reading Buddies isn't usually my thing," Izzy said, examining the clothes. "But you know." She jerked her chin at Noa. "Tractor beam."

"But, hey, Lucy knows you too," Noa said to Mal. "Why haven't I seen you here before?"

"Oh, I volunteered for Reading Buddies last spring," Mal explained. She reached up to unclip the fur and Noa waved their hands to stop her.

"Hang on! That one looks great!" Noa said. "You should keep it on." They hesitated. "You are helping with Reading Buddies today, right?"

"Oh," Mal said slowly. "Sure?" If the comic club kids were doing Reading Buddies anyway, she may as well. But Reading Buddies didn't usually involve costumes.

"Great!" Noa's smile grew even wider, and Mal noticed they had a dimple in one cheek. Okay, that was adorable. "Here, Izzy," Noa said, pushing a pair of sparkling fairy wings toward their friend. "You need some sparkle."

"I need sparkle like a fish needs wheels," Izzy said dryly. But she pulled the wings on over her gray sweater vest. "There," she said, waving her hands in the air half-heartedly. "Time to sparkle."

"Yesss!!!" Noa called out, tossing the blue boa around their neck. They struck a pose. "How do I look?"

"You look fabulous," Mal said, smiling back. She couldn't help it, even though she had no idea what was happening. Noa's smile made her want to smile too. Mal was having a hard time not noticing how cute Noa was. In a non-girl, non-boy way. *Don't think about that*, she told herself. *Remember, no more crushes this year.* What she should be thinking about was why she was wearing a costume. She opened her mouth to ask, but Noa was pointing at the bulk of her backpack under the fur.

"Leave your stuff here, if you want," they said. "And come on!"

"Um," Mal said. But Izzy's wings were disappearing out the door and Noa was hurrying after her. Without really thinking about it, Mal slid the backpack off her shoulder. She felt an immediate relief as the weight fell to the floor. But it was quickly replaced with a squirmy uncertainty in her stomach. What had she just gotten herself into?

Mallory Marsh was not a performer. In fact, Mallory Marsh could think of few things worse than a crowd of people looking at her. Noa, she could tell already, needed crowds like Mallory needed her sketchbook. And they seemed to be under the impression that Mallory felt the same way. This was going to be a disaster.

It wasn't. The only performance of any kind was from Shuga Toast, a gorgeous Black drag queen wearing a shimmery copper gown and a huge curly blond wig. Her brown skin sparkled with her signature body glitter, and tiny gems glimmered along the edges of her golden eye shadow. She held up a Pete the Cat book and tapped a long shiny fingernail on the words as she read, "'Pete stepped in a large pile of . . .'"

A little boy yelled out, "Stwabewies," and Shuga Toast gave him a huge smile.

"Strawberries, yes!" she agreed. "And what color did they turn his fabulous shoes?"

"Reeeedddd," chorused the kids in unison.

Then Mal noticed one woman who wasn't smiling. She stood in the back, and she kept glancing toward the kids sitting on the floor. None of the kids were misbehaving or anything. They were following along, calling out the colors when Shuga Toast asked. But the woman's forehead was scrunched in a frown, and just as Pete's shoes were washing back to white, she slipped from the room, her arms crossed tightly against her body.

Mal wondered what that had been about. But the kids were lining up to read with Shuga Toast one-on-one now, and she suddenly felt way too visible in the white fur.

Noa leaned toward her and grinned. "This is our moment, Mal the Magnificent," they said, tossing one end of the boa over their shoulder. Noa marched up to a little boy and crouched down to see the book he was holding. Izzy headed over to a little girl who had been staring at her fairy wings and they were soon reading a Tinkerbell book.

Mal let out a breath of relief that she wasn't expected to do some kind of dramatic production. Mal read with three kids before Reading Buddies ended. After the kids had all waved goodbye to Shuga Toast, one little girl came running back to give Mal a hug before leaving. She felt her heart warm.

When she looked up, Noa was grinning at her, that dimple tucked into their cheek and a bit of blue fluff from the feather boa stuck in their curls. Mal didn't think they had stopped smiling at all since they'd met.

As Mal left the room with Izzy and Noa, she noticed Lucy speaking to a customer over by the entrance. It was the woman who had left with her arms crossed tight. Mal couldn't see her face, but the woman was shaking her head as she turned and walked out the front door. Lucy watched her go and then turned back with a sigh.

"Lucy," Noa called out, bounding up to her. "Didn't I tell you Shuga Toast was the best?"

Lucy smiled, looking around at the kids and their grown-ups. "Yeah, she was fantastic. I just wish everyone appreciated it." There was a slight edge to her voice.

"What do you mean? Of course they did," Noa said. "See them?" They nodded toward a dad wearing a baby in a carrier and holding a little girl's hand. "That dad didn't even know what drag was when you invited them in. And I just heard him tell his kid they'd come back for the holiday performance!"

Izzy nodded. "I heard another mom talking about it too. She seemed excited."

Lucy brightened. "Oh? That is good news! I'm so glad they enjoyed it."

But now Noa was frowning. "Why'd you say that? Who didn't appreciate it? Did someone say something?"

"It's nothing," Lucy said quickly. "I shouldn't have let it

get to me." She gave Mal a friendly pat on the back. "It's so good to have you back, Mallory! I didn't see your name on my volunteer list."

"Oh." Mal hesitated. "I actually came for comic club."

"Really?" Noa said. "That's perfect! You can totally do both. I do!"

"I told you Noa would pull you in," Izzy said, struggling to remove her fairy wings.

"For the record," Noa told Izzy, "*you* pulled *me* into comic club."

"So when *is* comic club?" Mal asked. Mal's brain didn't usually process things quickly, and everything had been moving so fast since she met Noa. One moment she was lying to her coach about going to comic club. The next she was wearing a costume and reading with kids.

"We usually meet Mondays and Wednesdays. Today was Read with a Queen so I just really wanted to volunteer instead," Noa explained, helping Izzy take off the wings. "You should come! It's lots of fun. A bunch of us get together and talk about comics and anime and stuff."

"More like argue," Izzy said, tugging at her vest and taking the wings from Noa.

"We do not," Noa insisted. "We just express differing opinions." They tilted their head to the side, considering. Then they added, "Passionately."

"You realize that you two are arguing about whether or

not you argue, right?" Lucy said with a grin as she led them to her office.

Noa and Izzy looked at each other and laughed. Mal could feel the easy back-and-forth between them rolling like gentle waves. Usually, the very idea of arguing was enough to send Mal into an internal mini-panic. But this argument felt . . . different. Noa and Izzy seemed totally comfortable with each other, even while disagreeing. Comfortable enough that Izzy reached over and pulled the bit of blue fluff out of Noa's hair.

"Anyway, Mallory," Lucy said, turning to her. "We have a few kids in the comic club who like to help us out with Reading Buddies now and then. If you decide to volunteer officially, just have your mom fill in the online application."

"Sure, I'll tell her," Mal said, unclipping the fur and putting it back onto the hanger. As Lucy left the office, Izzy made a motion like she was reeling in a fishing line.

"*Not* what a tractor beam looks like," Noa said, pointing a finger at her.

Izzy snorted and then waved at Mal. "Nice to meet you, Mal," she said. "I gotta run. I'll see you on Wednesday." She backed out of the room, doing the reeling motion again.

Noa giggled. Then they looked at Mal.

"You don't have to do both comic club and Reading Buddies, though," Noa said. "Don't feel pressured. I know I can be a lot." Their eyebrows pulled together, like they were worried about whether Mal was just going along with them.

It was surprising. Most of the time, people were just happy that Mal did what they wanted.

"No, I want to," Mal said quickly. "I love comics! And I liked reading with kids today."

Noa's face cleared, and Mal felt another flutter as the blue-gray of their eyes lit up. As Mal left, pulling on her overstuffed backpack, Noa called after her, "See you in two days, Mal the Magnificent!"

As she walked up to the community center, Mal caught a glimpse of herself in the double glass doors. Her shaggy bangs hung too low over her glasses, and her denim jacket was covered in worn patches from all her favorite shows. There were no feathers or furs to hide behind. And the weight of her backpack was digging into her shoulders again. But she remembered what Noa had said about how she looked in the fur and couldn't help smiling at her reflection.

WHEN THE DISPOSAL AUTHORITY BOUGHT THE RUINED PLANET EARTH AFTER THE WAR, ARTIFICIAL INTELLIGENCE WAS IMMEDIATELY OUTLAWED.

ALL A.I. ROBOTS WERE DESTROYED, AND THE PARTS WERE SENT TO SALVAGE.

IF I CAN FIND ENOUGH OF THOSE ILLEGAL PARTS...

I MIGHT NOT BE SO ALONE ANYMORE.

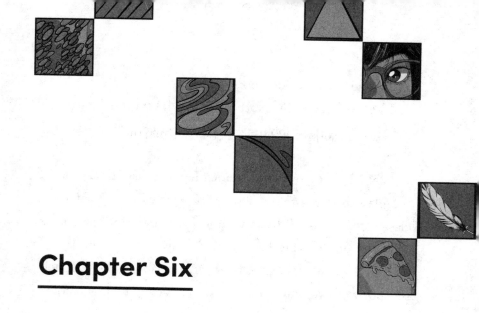

Chapter Six

IN ART CLASS, WHEN MISS HILL GAVE THEM TIME
to start on their self-portrait, Mal found herself absently
sketching a manga face on the back of a class handout instead.
She drew short curly hair that fell to one side in a lopsided
waterfall and she pressed down hard to make the line of the
eyelids extra dark. But it didn't quite capture Noa and those
eyes. She scrunched the paper into a ball and dropped it into
her backpack.

"Have you come up with any ideas, Mallory?"

Mal jumped. Miss Hill was walking over, her long box
braids swinging. She wore her usual kind smile and her skirt

printed with comic book pop art.

"Oh. No, not really. Nothing yet," Mal stammered.

"Have you tried looking at the adjective list?" Miss Hill asked.

Mal blinked, trying to remember the list. Everyone in the class had written a descriptive word for each of their classmates. Miss Hill had compiled the descriptions and at the start of class she had handed each of them the list of adjectives their classmates had written about them. Their self-portraits were supposed to incorporate all their adjectives in some way.

"Mallory, where is your list?" Miss Hill frowned, looking around. "You did get yours, didn't you?"

"Y-yes," Mal said quickly, scrambling around her desk. Where was her list? It had been here at the beginning of class. But Mallory had not even read the words on it. Her mind had been preoccupied and then she'd started sketching on a spare piece of paper. . . . *Oh.* She glanced at her backpack where she had dropped the crumpled drawing.

"I put it away," Mal said. "I wanted to take it home. So I could think about it some more." She gave her teacher a rueful smile. "I think I was just having a creative block today."

"Creative blocks happen," Miss Hill said. "You are sure you have your list, though?" She looked at Mal's bag. The bell rang just in time, and Mal hefted the bag to her shoulder.

"Yep, I have it. I'll look over it more tonight," she assured

Miss Hill before hurrying from the room.

At lunch, Etta was all worked up about some campaign her mom was involved in for fair housing options. Mal nodded and agreed and nodded and agreed while Etta explained it all fervently. She did her best to match Etta's indignation about the terrible state of housing inequality. Which, Mal had to agree, sounded pretty bad.

Etta disappeared as soon as the bell rang, and Mal headed to class. As she passed the lockers, she noticed Wendy trying to cram all her science project stuff into her locker. The door kept popping open. Mal saw Wendy glance at the clock on the wall and knew immediately she was worried about being late to her advanced math class.

"Just put it in mine," Mal said, opening her own locker.

Wendy looked from her armful of materials and notebooks to Mal's locker. "Are you sure?"

"I carry everything with me anyway," Mal said. "I like having it accessible." She tried not to think about how heavy her backpack felt. "My locker is your locker."

"Okay," Wendy said, hefting her things into the open locker. She arranged them inside and carefully closed the door, making sure it clicked shut. "Thanks, Mal!"

"No problem," Mal said. "What are friends for?"

Wendy answered her with a line from *Battlestar Galactica*. "'So say we all.'"

Mal repeated solemnly, "'So say we all.'" She turned and

nearly ran straight into Fiona.

"Yikes." Fiona stepped back, gripping her binder. Her blue eyes darted toward Wendy, who was already halfway down the hall. "What was all that about?" Fiona asked. "'So say we all'? Like, what is that?"

"Nothing, nothing," Mal said quickly. "It's just from a show."

"She is so weird sometimes," Fiona said. "I mean, totally in a good way!" she added quickly. "You are super nice, though." She linked her arm with Mal's as they walked toward class. "I don't know how you handle it."

"Um, thanks?" Mal said. She had the confusing sense that everything around her had shifted. A moment ago, Mal and Wendy had been talking side by side, and now it was as if Fiona had spun her around to look back at Wendy from a distance. It gave her an uncomfortable, nagging feeling, like she should be sticking up for Wendy.

Before she could figure out what to say, Fiona leaned toward her and whispered, "Hey, you missed swim yesterday! Coach had Dinesh demonstrate the butterfly for us."

"Who's Dinesh?" Mal asked.

"Cutie number one!" Fiona elbowed her. "You're coming today, right? You do *not* want to miss the chance to just openly stare at him for fifty meters."

"Oh, I'll definitely be there!" Mal said.

They stepped into their classroom, giggling. As Mal slid

into her seat, she locked eyes with Etta. She was staring at Mal with that green-eyed Etta concentration that made her feel like she was under a microscope. Fiona walked across to her own seat and Mal busied herself with pulling things from her backpack.

"Why do you do that?" Etta asked. She didn't sound upset, but Mal felt herself pulling away inside.

"Do what?" she asked.

"With Fiona, you . . ." Etta tapped her chin thoughtfully. "Switch."

"Switch?" Mal asked. She pulled out a pencil with a broken tip and her Totoro sharpener. There was a creeping feeling on the back of her neck, and she could feel the itch to shut down and sink into that dark cave inside her.

"It just seems like you aren't yourself around her," Etta went on, still looking at Mal with those intense eyes. "You were actually playing with your hair when you came in. Like a Fiona-Mal hybrid."

Mal shoved her pencil into the sharpener and turned it, not saying anything. *Leave me alone, Etta,* she thought. Why did it matter if she acted like Fiona sometimes? It didn't hurt anyone.

"Fiona's not that bad," Mal said mildly, focused on her pencil. "She's changed, you know. She's way nicer now."

"That's not what I'm saying," Etta said, but then class started and Mal, relieved, put the conversation behind her.

She didn't have time to worry about whether Etta thought she acted too much like Fiona. Right now she needed all her focus to grasp these math concepts.

Mallory meant to talk to Mom that night. She'd already skipped one swim practice and if she didn't tell her mom soon, things would get complicated. But that night her brain felt lost in a fog. She had so much homework and so little energy. *Maybe*, she told herself, *once I've gotten some homework done, I'll be ready to talk to Mom.* Just as she was about to open the online calculator and work on her math, Mal decided to peek at Comic Koala. She loved the online site almost as much as the real-life shop. When she'd first started following webcomics, Mal had gotten pulled into some online fandoms that got real toxic, real fast. Whenever people started yelling at each other in the comments, Mal's skin would crawl and her stomach would hurt. But Comic Koala was different. S.J. Summerhill made sure to keep things civil.

Mal only meant to take a quick look before math, just to see if the webcomic she'd uploaded over the weekend had gotten many comments. But splashed across the home page was a speech bubble with bold letters that read:

Comic Koala November Competition! Vote for your favorite webcomic! Winners in multiple categories! Winning comics featured on home page, cash prizes, professional consultation from S.J.theBoss! (publication not guaranteed).

Mal sucked in her breath, reading each line again and again. *A competition.* Comic Koala had done this once before. The winner of last years' Best Comic had gone on to sign a book deal for a graphic novel.

Mal clicked on the announcement and her eyes flew down to the page of competition rules until she found what she wanted. *Categories.* Mal knew her webcomic wasn't nearly as good as others. There were adults who had studied this stuff and who sold advertising on their pages because they had so much web traffic. But for a twelve-and-a-half-year-old, Mal was killing it. She had thousands of subscribers. That had to count for something.

There, she thought, her heart beating faster as she read. *Category: Amateur webcomic artist, youth (13–16 year-olds).* According to the made-up birth date she had picked when she first created her account, Dr.BotGirl was nearly fourteen. She was solidly in the amateur youth category.

The notifications icon blinked in the corner of her screen and Mal clicked on it. Besides the usual hearts and the comments, a "vote" option had been added. Mal felt a thrill tingle through her entire body. Dr.BotGirl already had 253 votes. She clicked back to the competition page and read over the words again, a smile stretching across her face. If she won, her comic would be featured on the front page, and she'd have a chance to talk to S.J. Summerhill about actually publishing her comics! The smile slipped. No, wait. She couldn't do that.

Mal couldn't meet with S.J. Summerhill. There was probably some legal reason why S.J. would need to talk to Mal's parents. The elation that had carried her the last few minutes whooshed out of Mal like air from a punctured balloon. She slumped in her seat. If she won the Comic Koala competition and S.J. contacted her parents, none of that would matter. All they would care about was that she had lied.

Then her eyes landed on "cash prizes." Could it be enough cash to make a difference? She imagined her mom storming in, demanding to know if she had lied about her age to post webcomics. *"Yes, Mom,"* she'd admit tearfully. *"But I did it for us."* And then she'd pull out wads of cash and hand them to her mother. *"See, Mom?"* she'd say. *"You don't have to work extra anymore. I've got you."*

"Oh, Mallory," Mom would say, clutching the bills to her chest. *"Gomawo! You've saved our family!"*

"Mallory!"

Mal jumped and slammed the laptop shut. Her mom's voice outside her door called out, "Time for bed!"

"Okay, Mom," she called, shoving the laptop away. It was a ridiculous fantasy. Mal couldn't solve Mom's problems by winning a competition. But as she got ready for bed, she couldn't help thinking that maybe there was something to it. If she won a cash prize, Mom wouldn't just throw that away. She would have to admit, finally, that Mal's doodling might actually be worthwhile.

Chapter Seven

MALLORY MARSH KNEW EXACTLY HOW TO MAKE people like her. All she had to do was pay attention. If someone in the group seemed like the leader, Mal would make sure they knew she wasn't a threat, laughing along with their jokes and never interrupting them. If someone talked too much, Mal would be the one who listened to their stories. She was friendly to the loners and polite to the adults. She could fit herself easily into any group. She just had to analyze the situation.

As she walked into the library on Wednesday, Mal thought of herself as one of Zee's robots, scanning the kids in comic club to figure out what each of them were like and what each of them wanted from her. But as soon as her eyes locked on Noa, Mal forgot to be analytical. Yesterday, Mal had the strange feeling that maybe Noa wasn't even real. But the moment she saw Noa, she couldn't imagine anyone more real. They wore a denim romper and sat perched on a tall stool, deep in the middle of an animated discussion. Their hands moved as they talked, and even from a distance, Mal knew they were wearing that dark eyeliner again. She walked forward, unable to take her eyes off Noa. *Tractor beam*, said a voice in her head. Izzy had been right about that.

Just then Izzy's voice interrupted Noa. "It doesn't make any sense, though." Izzy pointed at a book on the table in front of her as she talked. "In the manga he doesn't even go to prison. So he's never punished for his actions? He's just forgiven after everything he did? It's totally unfair!"

"It's not about fair!" Noa leaned forward, practically sliding off the edge of their seat. "Naruto had to forgive him. What kind of a story would it be otherwise?"

"He didn't deserve it," said a firm voice. Mal blinked at the boy who had spoken. She knew him from LPA. He was a huge white boy, towering over all the other kids in their class, even P.J. She'd seen him with P.J., come to think of it. He was the guy that P.J. and Brett called Fizz. "Sasuke was evil," the big boy said, nodding his head like he'd made a definitive statement.

A skinny Black boy with cornrows threw out his hands. "But he didn't actually *do* that much evil. He mostly just *talked* about doing bad stuff."

Mal's eyes widened as she caught a glimpse of his face. She knew him too. He was the tall boy in the hall, the one who had posted the flyer. She stopped walking, her heart pounding in her chest. Did he know about *Metal-Plated Heart*? Did the rest of them?

"Hey, it's Mallory the Magnificent!" Noa slid completely off their stool and rushed over to her. "You came." They smiled, their face all warmth and light, and Mal felt the panicky feeling fade away.

"I told you," Mal said. "I love comics."

Noa linked their arm through hers and pulled her over to the table. "Come meet everyone!"

"Excellent," Izzy said, leaning back and eyeing Mallory. "You are exactly what we need."

Mal gave her an uncertain smile. "Oh, great," she said. What did Izzy mean by that?

"You're totally right," the kid with the cornrows said, bouncing up and down. He was wearing dangling earrings that swayed as he moved. "We needed one more person!"

Mal kept smiling, trying to read the eager faces looking her way. She liked being needed. But who exactly did they need her to be?

Then the big kid grunted one word. "Tiebreaker."

Mal's stomach sank. She looked at Noa, who was still grinning.

"You like Naruto?" Noa asked. Mal nodded slowly. "Perfect," Noa said, pulling Mal closer and positioning her at the head of the table. "So," they said, "should Naruto have forgiven Sasuke? Yes?" Noa jumped to the side of the table where the boy with the earrings was still bouncing excitedly. "Or no?" they said, gesturing to the other side, where Izzy sat with her arms crossed next to the big kid.

Mal swallowed. She looked at the two sides facing off and wanted to crawl under the table. Of all the things they could have asked her to be, why did it have to be a tiebreaker?

"Um," she stalled.

The bouncing boy scrunched up his forehead. "You know what we're talking about, right? We didn't, like, spoil the whole manga for you? Or the anime, if that's your thing?"

"I know them both," Mal said, thinking. She could side with Noa on the yes side. She wanted to make Noa happy. But . . . her eyes landed on Fizz. She imagined disagreeing with him. How mad would he get? Would he tell his friends, like P.J. and Brett? Would they come after her if she picked the wrong side of the discussion at a stupid club she should never have even joined? Mal looked down at her shoes miserably. "I don't think I have an opinion."

All four of them stared at her for a moment.

"Well, that's new," Izzy said with a little snort. Then she

shrugged. "Okay. Introductions, then?"

Mal blinked.

"Yep," Noa agreed, hopping back onto their stool. The boy sat down too, grinning at Mal. He waved at the chair in front of her. She hesitated, bewildered at how quickly they had moved on. These kids had told her exactly what they wanted from her and she had failed them. Immediately. She had never so completely messed up at meeting a new group of people. But they still seemed to want her there. Even Fizz was looking at her expectantly. Or was that menacingly? Mal slid her backpack off her shoulders and sat down, dropping it on the floor next to her. She rolled her stiff shoulders.

"Okay, so, I'm Marcus," the boy with the cornrows said. "He/him. I've seen you at school, I think." Mal nodded. "I love comics," Marcus continued. "Superhero stuff is cool but I'm really all about the manga and the anime. And this is my fellow blerd Izzy," he added, shooting finger guns at Izzy.

Izzy rolled her eyes. "I can introduce myself, *blerd*." She saw Mal's confused look and explained, "he means Black nerd. But I'm a way cooler nerd than Marcus."

"Rude," Marcus said, his voice cracking on the word. But he didn't seem offended.

"Izzy. She/her," Izzy said. "Actually, Mal and I go way back." She tipped her chin up at Mal in a nod. "Glad you came."

"We met Monday," Noa added. They threw out their

arms. "Remember me, Mal?"

"Yeah, yes. I do," Mal said, thinking of Noa's floppy hat and the fluffy boa. And that adorable dimple. "Hi, Noa," she said. Noa grinned and Mal looked away, flustered.

"Um, I know you already too," Mal said, tilting her head back to look up at the big kid sitting next to her. "We go to LPA together. Hi, Fizz."

"No." His voice was softer than Mal expected.

"You . . . don't go to LPA?" Mal said.

"Not Fizz," the boy corrected her.

"That's James," Marcus said. There was a flicker of worry on his face as he said it and his smile looked tense. Mal looked back at James. His eyebrows were scrunched in a frown.

"Oh, hi, James," Mal said carefully. Had she upset him? Was he going to snap her in two with his massive hands? "I didn't know that was your name."

"Because of those jerks at school," Marcus said, looking annoyed. "They just make up nicknames for people. They never ask anyone if they like it."

"Oh," Mal said. P.J. used nicknames for lots of people. She'd assumed this kid was friends with him and didn't mind. "Sorry, James," she said. "I'll make sure to remember your name at school."

The frown cleared, and James gave her a small smile. Marcus clapped his hands together and declared, "I like her. She can stay."

Izzy rolled her eyes again. Noa loudly pointed out that it was never up to Marcus. And suddenly the entire table was arguing again. Even when the conversation switched back to comics, it never stopped being an argument. Mal had never been in a group that argued this much. And she'd definitely never enjoyed it. She'd only ever talked about this stuff online. It was fun to know kids IRL who wanted to talk about whether Goku had too much power. No one seemed to hold any of the disagreements against anyone else either. Mal found herself joining in and by the time the club ended, she felt almost a part of things.

"Hey," Izzy said as Mal stood up and hefted her backpack off the floor. "Did you do that Kiki painting on your jacket?"

"Oh. Yeah," Mal said. Mal hadn't been able to find an iron-on patch from *Kiki's Delivery Service* for her denim jacket. So instead she had used fabric paint to make her own picture of the little witch with her cat perched on the broom handle as they flew through the air.

"Nice!" Noa said, delighted. "You're really good. Next time we should look at everyone's art. Well, not mine, but everyone else here is super talented."

"Really?" Mal asked. Marcus had just left, and James had gone looking for a comic book, but Mal remembered seeing sketchbooks in front of both of them. She thought about the sketches on the flyer.

"I do hand lettering more than drawing," Izzy said. "I like

playing with fonts and calligraphy and stuff. But Marcus and James are both really good with pictures. I keep telling them we should start a webcomic."

"Oh," Mal said. "Do you like webcomics?" She hoped her voice sounded normal.

"Yeah. Have you heard of this site called Comic Koala?"

Mal's mouth went dry, but Izzy kept talking. "It's connected to the comic shop. But it's a whole online webcomic community. You can read people's comics and vote on them and stuff."

"*We* can't. None of us are thirteen yet," Noa said.

"I told you, we just need an adult to do it for us," Izzy said. "I bet someone here would." She looked around. The only staff member in sight was Barbara, an older white librarian who was glaring down two boys who had been running by the desk.

"Yeah, go ask her," Noa said, grinning at Izzy.

"Barbara the Brutal? No way." Izzy made a face.

As she shouldered her backpack and left, Mal felt the weight of her sketchbook and all the secrets inside it digging into her shoulders. She couldn't show the comic club her sketchbook, especially since they already knew about Comic Koala. Two of these kids went to LPA. No matter how comfortable she got with these kids, she couldn't let them find out about Dr.BotGirl.

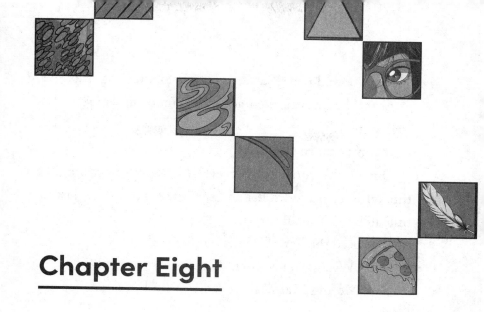

Chapter Eight

MAL HAD A COUCH CUSHION OVER HER HEAD AND the volume on her music turned up to an unhealthy level on her headphones. But she still couldn't drown out the lightsaber battle happening around her. She desperately wanted to shut herself away in her room and rewatch *My Hero Academia*. But Mom's Babysitting Rule #1 was *Never leave the double Ws unsupervised.* Her phone buzzed. She lifted the corner of the cushion and peeked down at the screen.

 Mom: Sorry, sweetie, running behind!
 Won't be done for another 20 probably.
 Or 30.

Mal allowed herself a tiny groan before texting back, *No problem*. She paused, then added a thumbs-up emoji and a smiley emoji.

Mom: You're the best!

Out of the corner of her eye, Mal saw something fly through the air toward her and she lifted the cushion just in time to block a small slipper.

"She used the Force!" Winston shouted.

"No," Wyatt shouted back. "Because I'm the Jedi!"

"No! Me and Mal-Mal are Jedis," Winston said. "You are Sift."

"*Sith*," Wyatt corrected him.

"Sift is what I said!"

Mal decided it was time to break Mom's Babysitting Rule #2: *No screens after dinner*.

"Who wants to watch *The Clone Wars*?" she called.

With the twins finally settled in front of the TV, Mal grabbed her homework and opened her laptop. She stared at the math problems, wishing for Zee's cybernetic eye that could scan and process info immediately. Mal's phone buzzed again. It was her dad, and Mal knew even before he said it that he was canceling his weekend with them.

Dad: Hey, Pumpkin. I'm going to have to work this weekend. I'm sorry.

Mal: that's okay. Work is work!

Dad: I could make it up to you by picking up you and the boys after swim? I could take you out for pizza?

Mal: yeah, that sounds great! ☺

Dad: How about Monday?

Mal bit her lip. It would be so awkward if Dad showed up at swim on Monday and she wasn't there.

Mal: Can it be Tuesday?

Dad: Monday and Wednesday are the only days I can next week.

Mal: Could we save it for after Thanksgiving? I have a lot of homework the next couple weeks.

Dad: What are you working on?

Mal: Math

Dad: Way to be responsible. OK, we'll wait on that pizza. Go get sum work done.

Mal: Dad

Dad: get it? Sum? Math?

Mal: DAD

Dad: ok, ok. Love you, Pumpkin.

Mal: love you dad ♥

Mal wasn't exactly trying to be sneaky. She *did* have a lot of math homework. Mal looked at her screen and felt her brain balk. *I'll just take a quick break*, she told herself as she pulled up the Comic Koala site.

Her face lit up as she glanced over the notifications. She had another 240 votes since posting her newest episode. If she could keep posting new content, Dr.BotGirl would have a good chance in this competition. She scrolled through the votes, a warm, glowing feeling in her chest. Then she saw a new comment.

It was on episode ten, her most popular one. It was the episode where Zee and her crew finally get the city to offer sanctuary to the refugees gathered outside. Zee, undercover as universal superstar Zelda Silver, has just performed her song about inclusion and the residents have thrown open the city gates to welcome in the alien refugees. Mal's eyes skimmed over the final frame in the comic, the scene with the giant holographic message *You Belong* hovering over the crowd silhouetted below.

She scrolled down to the new comment. There were only three words but they sent chills down Mal's spine. "This looks familiar."

Mallory Marsh had plenty of unhealthy habits. She ate too much sugar, she was allergic to saying no, and despite her giant eco-friendly water bottle, she didn't hydrate enough. But the one thing she always absolutely rocked was a good night's sleep. She could fall asleep as easily in Wendy's creaky attic room or in the room that Etta shared with her little sister as she could in her own. But tonight that comment glowed bright in her mind, keeping her awake. The last frame in episode ten was modeled exactly after the mural Etta had painted on the wall at school. A crowd was silhouetted along the bottom, all with different hairstyles and clothing, stars shining above them and the words "You Belong" in big letters. The crowd in her webcomic was made up of aliens and robots instead of LPA students. But it was similar enough. And someone had recognized it.

It was a brand-new profile—no other comments, no posts, not even an avatar. Mallory tossed and turned in her bed. Her brain kept circling. It could be that one girl in art who drew cartoons or that boy who wore Naruto shirts. Izzy and Noa didn't go to LPA, so they wouldn't have recognized the mural. But it could be Marcus. He had posted the flyer with drawings that looked like her characters. Or even James.

Sleep was not happening. Maybe Mal just needed a snack. There was leftover mac and cheese in the fridge. And there was still a container of kimchi that she could mix in. Her mouth watered at the thought. Mal padded downstairs, trying to be extra quiet. But when she got to the bottom of the stairs, Mal heard her mom's voice in the living room.

She froze. Was Mom talking to Dad? There was no way. He came in the house only long enough to pick the kids up or drop them off. Her parents were not on late-night-chat terms. There was a pause before her mom spoke again, and Mal realized she was speaking English mixed with Korean, which meant she was probably on the phone with Emo Sue, Mal's aunt in Sacramento. Mal should have gone back upstairs right then, except that it sounded like her mom—her powerful, workaholic, organized, perfect mom—was crying.

"And I obviously don't mind at all when they stay here on the weekend." Her mom sniffled.

Mal realized what this was about. Dad had started traveling a lot for work in the past year. After he moved out, Mal had hoped he'd change his schedule, maybe pick them up from school some days. Instead, her parents had decided the kids would just spend every other weekend at Dad's apartment. But they hadn't been there in a couple weeks.

"So he gives me a whole story about how he's going to take them out for dinner Monday night to make up for it. Then you know what he does?" Mom's voice had an edge to it that made Mal's shoulders tense. "Messages me tonight saying that won't work either. Big surprise."

Mal's stomach twisted into a guilty pretzel. *She* had told Dad not to come meet them on Monday. It wasn't Dad's fault that Mom was upset. It was hers. She took a step backward up the stairs. She wished she hadn't heard any of this.

"Now he's asking if we can alternate weekends because he's having such a hard time with this *adjustment*." Mom sighed and blew her nose. "Mianhae. I'm a mess. Don't tell

Umma. You know what she'll say."

It was definitely Mal's aunt on the phone. Only she and Mom called Mal's grandma Umma. Mal took another backward step, willing the stairs not to squeak.

"Oh, not you too." Mom's words sounded sharp. "You know how hard Dan and I have worked to keep things stable for the kids during all this. I'm not going to drag them across the country. We're doing fine here."

Mal's foot froze halfway to the next step. *Drag them across the country?*

"I know you would but—" Mom's voice cut off and Mal knew her aunt was talking again. Now she wished she *could* hear. Was Mom thinking about moving? To California? Mom had grown up in Columbus, but she had a lot of family in Sacramento. After Mal's grandpa passed away, her halmoni had moved there to live with Emo Sue and her family. Mal missed Halmoni and she loved going to visit her and Emo Sue's family. But she didn't want to move there.

"We *are* fine," Mom said, her voice insistent. "So you can tell Umma to stop asking me what the kids are eating." She gave a choked laugh. "Umma talks like they're going to starve if I don't have time to make a full-course meal every day."

Mal swallowed hard. She wasn't hungry anymore. The thought of moving to Sacramento had ruined her appetite. And what about Dad? They'd already gone from seeing him every day to once a week, sometimes less. His whole family lived in Ohio. There was no way he'd move to California.

"Oh, she's been wonderful. I don't know what I'd do without her. She's so responsible and organized. And so good with the twins."

Mal leaned forward, straining to hear. She couldn't help it. Her mom had to be talking about her.

"She *is* my Mini-Me. I can't tell you what a relief it is to have something in my life I don't have to worry about."

Her mom didn't worry about her. That was . . . good. Mal didn't want her mom to worry, especially about her. So why did the lump in her throat hurt so much?

"Besides, I couldn't take her away from her school. She's doing so well. And swim team! She's been on that same team for years. I would never take her away from something she loves so much, especially after everything she does for me."

Everything Mom said made Mal's stomach drop another notch, like an elevator going down from floor to floor. Mom didn't want to take Mal away from LPA because she was doing so well. If she knew how much Mal was struggling in math, would she change her mind? And if Mom knew she hated swim team, would it make sense to take her away from it and move her across the country?

Mom changed the subject, her voice taking on an upbeat quality as she asked Emo Sue about her kids. Mal's throat stung and her eyes were starting to prickle. She tiptoed the rest of the way upstairs and back into bed. Her mom was so proud of Mal's responsibility and her organization and of all the things she thought were true of Mal. But they weren't. Not really. Mal was responsible and organized *for Mom. Because* of Mom. Around her mom, Mal morphed into someone who loved swimming competitively and always did her homework and fed her brothers dinner at exactly six o'clock. Because that was who Mom needed her to be. But it wasn't her. She hated competition and getting yelled at by Coach Perkins. Homework was fine, until she didn't feel like it or she got sucked into her webcomic, and then it was so hard to get back on track. She was so behind in math that the thought of doing any of it made her feel like she was caught in a trash compactor, the walls slowly moving in to crush her. And she wasn't the one who made to-do lists and schedules. That was Mom.

Mal pulled the covers over her head, tears trickling down her cheeks. Her mom worked so hard and seemed so invincible. But tonight Mom sounded like she was breaking. And if Mom broke any more, she might decide it would be easier just to move to where her family could help with things. To Sacramento. Mal wiped her face on her sheets and sat up. Her family needed her to keep being responsible and organized, like the person that Mom bragged about on the phone. She had a sudden image of a sticky name tag with

"Perfect Daughter" written on it. That was who she had to be. Or her mom might fall apart.

Mal reached for her Chromebook. A few weeks ago, Mom had logged in to her email on Mal's Chromebook when her laptop died during a virtual meeting. Mal clicked on the login and started typing her mom's email, holding her breath. The password autofilled. Mal's heart sped up and she stared at the row of dots. *This might work*, she thought with a rush of adrenaline. She hit Enter. Her mom's inbox opened on the screen. Mal did a quick search for "library" and scrolled until she found an old email from Lucy. She copied Lucy's email address into a new message and typed: "Hi, Mal is volunteering for Reading Buddies and that's fine."

Mal looked at the message and bit her lip, thinking about how her mom talked to other adults. She changed a few words, erased some others, and added an ending. "Hello, Mallory will be volunteering for Reading Buddies occasionally if that works for you! Thanks so much. Take care, Magnolia."

Before she could reconsider, Mal hit Send. Almost immediately she felt her chest clench in panic. What if Lucy responded? Her mom would see and know she had hacked into her email. She would never trust Mallory again— *Stop*, Mal told herself sternly. She took a long deep breath. She could do this. She just had to be the kind of person who knew how to cover their tracks. In her webcomic, Zee's turtle-shaped hovership was controlled by an intelligent super-computer called Tack. What would Tack do if Zee needed to hack someone's email? *A filter*, whispered a voice in her head. Perfect.

Mal selected Lucy's email address and set a filter to send any emails from her to spam. A tingle of satisfaction began to replace the worry in Mal's stomach. She was solving problems, just like her characters. Just like Zee. She went to the library website and found the volunteer application. At the end, after putting in all her info, there was an official little checkbox she had to click. For moment, she almost couldn't do it. But she steeled herself, channeling the courage of Zee, and clicked.

Mal typed "swim team" in her mom's inbox next. She pulled up Coach Perkins's email and started to type a message, explaining that Mallory would be missing swim two days a week. Then she froze, her fingers hovering over the keyboard. Why stop at two days? Her brothers were signed up for aftercare. Noa had said they hung out at the library most days. Without swim, Mal could see Noa every day. Her heart sped up at the thought of that freedom.

She took a shaky, excited breath and typed, "Unfortunately, due to previous commitments, Mallory will no longer be able to participate in swim team. Thank you." She hit Send. She set a filter for Coach Perkins's email as well, just in case he emailed back. Then Mal closed her mom's inbox and shut the Chromebook.

Mal let out a deep breath. She'd done it. She'd fixed everything. It was a good feeling, like getting a lot of likes on her webcomic. It felt powerful. And she hadn't disappointed her mom at all. *Perfect Daughter, check.*

Chapter Nine

MAL KEPT CHECKING HER WEBCOMIC ALL
weekend, but there were no other weird comments. And her
votes kept climbing. Comic Koala had started a tracking
system that showed which webcomics were in the top five
of each category and Mal's was already in fourth place under
"Amateur: youth." She felt a little thrill every time she looked
at the numbers. So what if sniffy Mr. Emerson didn't think
Metal-Plated Heart was a "real story"? Thousands of readers
did, and that's what mattered. She posted a new episode on
Sunday night with an evil Disposal Authority official who
wore bow ties and glasses and sniffed when he talked.

Marcus wanted to do a drawing session at comic club on Monday, and Mal felt her stomach sink. The last thing she wanted was for kids from school to recognize her art. So when Noa left early to help with Reading Buddies, Mal jumped up too. Reading with kids seemed safer.

Soon they were both settled into the cushy lime-green chairs with books and squirmy kids. The little girl who wanted Mal to read *Pinkalicious* didn't even make it through half the book before her attention span ran out. Mal got paired with a second grader next who just needed a bit of help with some of the words. Mal gave her a high five and a sticker when they were done, but no one else was waiting. She found herself watching Noa. They were reading a book about trucks with a little boy who kept sliding off the chair. Noa read each truck with a different voice, obviously trying to keep his attention. His big blue eyes would stare up at Noa with each new voice, but then he'd look away and slide off the chair again.

"Hey, buddy," Noa said, "do you want a different book?"

Instantly, the boy jumped up and ran over to the stack of books next to Mal. He reached straight for *Pinkalicious* and ran back to Noa, climbing eagerly into the chair. He didn't even try to slide down again. When they were done and Noa offered him a sticker, he shook his head. Instead he reached for the book and clutched it to his chest.

"You want to check that book out?" Noa asked. They

stood up and reached for his hand. "Let's see if your grown-up has your library card."

He slipped his hand into Noa's, still holding *Pinkalicious* close, and looked around. "Mama!" he called out in a clear little voice. A woman standing to the side looked up from her phone. He pulled Noa over to his mom and held up the book. "I buy dis one," he said.

"We borrow library books, Davey," his mom said, reaching for it. "We don't buy them. Oh, Davey. No, not this one." She shook her head at the cover and tucked it behind another book on the shelf. "Let's find something else."

"No!" Davey reached for the book. "I want Pink!"

"Here." His mom pulled a superhero book from the shelf. "It's Batman. You love Batman!"

"*Pinkwishous!*" Davey said.

Noa looked down at Davey's small hand in theirs and then up at his mom. "He . . . he really likes that book," Noa said.

"No, he doesn't," Davey's mom said. "He's just used to pink everything. He has three older sisters." She sighed. "We don't need any more girl books, you know?"

"Um," Noa said. "Not really." Their voice was small and not at all like them. Mal had never seen Noa look uncertain before.

The mom's smile faltered. Her eyes narrowed slightly, as if she were really looking at Noa for the first time. Mal watched the mom take in Noa's long-sleeved men's shirt, the boys'

100

shorts, the pink tights, the nail polish, and earring. "Oh," the mom said. "Well." She smiled again, a little too big. "We'll get both, okay, Davey?" She grabbed *Pinkalicious* from where she had put it and motioned for Davey to follow her. "Let's go get our books!"

Davey let go of Noa's hand and followed his mom, grinning happily. His mom pointed back at Noa. "Say thank you to the nice . . ." she trailed off, flustered.

"Thank you," Davey said dutifully, and they headed to the checkouts.

Noa walked over and plopped onto the cushy chair next to Mal.

"You okay?" Mal asked.

Noa shrugged. "Did you catch all that?"

Mal nodded. "It was . . . awkward."

"Yeah," Noa said. "I confuse people sometimes. And that's okay, it's just . . ." They picked at their purple nail polish. "I don't always have the right things to say. Like, why didn't I just go, 'Colors don't have gender.'"

"Seriously," Mal said. "Colors are just colors. Books are just books. Why make it weird?"

Noa laughed. "Exactly!" They looked at Mal and asked quietly, "So, you're not confused by me?"

"No, of course not!" Mal said. "I mean, you're Noa." She'd only known Noa for a few days, but they were so clearly and completely themself. But Mal thought about that woman not knowing whether to call Noa a boy or a girl. And the look in Noa's eyes after. Maybe Noa wasn't as confident as they seemed. "Just be you," Mal said. "You don't need some kind of label."

Noa shrugged. "I kind of like labels," they said. "I'm nonbinary and that feels really good to say because for so long I didn't know how to explain myself."

"Oh." Mal bit her lip. "Yeah, I guess that makes sense." She looked around. Lucy was reading with the last Reading Buddies kid and Barbara was searching the shelf for a book, her eyebrows pulled together in concentration. Mal lowered her voice. "Are most people here cool, though? With . . . everything?"

"With me being nonbinary?" Noa asked, and their face lit up again. "Oh, totally. You know Zachary? The manager? He asked my pronouns when I started volunteering and I was like, *yes*, I am in the right place! Everyone's cool about it."

"Even Barbara the Brutal?" Mal asked, glancing toward the librarian.

Noa followed her gaze. Barbara stood behind the desk, one finger pressed into the cover of a book while she talked to a customer. Mal couldn't see her face, but she'd seen her give book recommendations before, her gold wire-frame glasses pushed up into her graying hair and her eyebrows drawn down. Mal herself had checked out books just because she was afraid to say no to Barbara. To be fair, Mal didn't like saying no to anyone.

"I do kind of feel like she glares at me whenever she uses my pronouns, but that might just be her normal setting?" Noa said.

"Yeah," Mal agreed. "I think that switch has been stuck on grumpy since the nineties."

Noa snorted so loud that Barbara turned and looked at them. Noa tried to swallow their laugh instead and started coughing. That set Mal off and soon both were curled over, covering their mouths to hide their giggles.

"No, they really are cool here," Noa said when they had settled down a bit. "When I asked Zachary if they could do drag story time, I really didn't know if they'd go for it."

"The drag queen thing was your idea?" Mal asked.

"Yeah! I saw Shuga Toast at a festival this summer and she was so good with kids and stuff. Oh, and did I tell you? We are planning a big drag queen Holiday Story Time for after Thanksgiving! Isn't that fun?"

Noa's eyes sparkled, and Mal could feel herself expanding toward them, like a balloon. Noa seemed to think she was the kind of person who loved over-the-top costumes and performances. The kind of person who would definitely love drag. Mal nodded. "Yeah, drag is super fun."

"Drag *is* fun," Noa agreed, "but it's so much more than that." They leaned their head against the back of the chair and looked at the ceiling. "I mean, both my moms are wildly okay with who I am. But there are so many people who aren't or who just don't get it. And . . . I don't know. I guess drag just lets people be whoever they want to be. No matter what everyone else thinks." They chewed on a purple fingernail. "I mean, how many kids out there don't have a chance to, like, try out different parts of themselves? Like read a frikkin pink book if they want?"

Mal thought about Davey and the way he clutched *Pinkalicious* to his chest. Her brothers had always loved all kinds of dress-up, including making dresses or skirts from blankets. Sometimes Winston asked her to paint his nails. But they were in kindergarten now. Was that why he hadn't asked her for a manicure lately? Had someone told him boys didn't wear nail polish?

"So drag queens coming here," Noa continued, "reading to kids and singing with them, and just being who they are . . . It feels like a chance. A chance for kids to see all kinds of people as normal, not . . ." Their voice trailed off a bit and they said quietly, "Not weird."

"You aren't weird," Mal said earnestly. "Well, I mean, unless you want to be. Because there's obviously nothing wrong with weird."

"I mean, people might *say* weird is fine," Noa said. Their eyebrows were drawn down and one of their yellow Converse high-tops was bouncing up and down. "But if a man puts on a dress and makeup, well, that's not the kind of weird they like so much."

Mal nodded. She thought about Fiona saying Wendy was weird for liking *Battlestar Galactica*. Why did the different parts of who you were get labeled normal or weird? Who decided that? And why couldn't there be more places where you could just try on all the different parts of yourself?

Chapter Ten

THE KIDS AT COMIC CLUB WERE DEEP IN A HEATED argument when Mal arrived on Wednesday. Noa waved at her, and James and Izzy nodded hello. Marcus looked up and stopped in the middle of a sentence.

"Hey, Mal," he said. "*None* of us agree about Miyazaki's best film. Can you believe it?"

"Uh, yeah, I think I can," Mal admitted with a grin.

"Wait!" Marcus said, his eyes suddenly bright. "Nobody tell Mal which is their favorite. Let's see if she agrees with anyone. Mal, which Miyazaki movie is number one?"

Four pairs of eyes turned to Mallory.

Mal bit her lip, looking at each one of them. "Well," she said slowly. "I mean, you can't go wrong with Miyazaki. They're all great. . . ." Four faces frowned back at her, and Mal knew immediately that they wanted an answer. Not having an opinion on this would be worse than disagreeing with someone. "I . . . I like *Nausicaä of the Valley of the Wind*," she said.

Noa grinned. James nodded thoughtfully. Marcus clapped his hands together. "See! We all have totally different favorites," he said. "We are a perfect mix."

"*Nausicaä* is good," Izzy admitted. "It's probably second to *Howl's Moving Castle* for me."

"But *Spirited Away*—" Marcus began.

"Is such a predictable choice," Izzy interrupted.

They all started talking at once, and the volume climbed. The sound of someone clearing their throat cut through the noise. Barbara stood there, her arms crossed over her chest and her watery-blue eyes glaring behind her wire-frame glasses.

"If you wish to continue meeting as a club here," Barbara said, "then you need to be aware of your volume. We can hear your opinions all across the library."

Mal slid down in her chair and Marcus hunched his shoulders. Even James seemed to shrink. Barbara started to turn away, then added, "Besides, the only correct answer is *Princess Mononoke*."

There was a moment of silence and then the table erupted in whispered comments and muffled laughter. Marcus slapped the table, delighted, and James turned all the way around to stare after Barbara as she returned to the desk.

"That is also an excellent choice," Izzy admitted. "Barbara the Brutal coming in with a surprise twist."

"Maybe Brutal isn't the best word for her," Noa said, tapping their chin. "I think there is more to Barbara than meets the eye."

"Oh, guess what?" Marcus leaned forward, lowering his voice conspiratorially. "Remember Comic Koala, the online site Izzy told us about?"

Mal swallowed hard as everyone around the table nodded. Of course they all knew about it.

"Well, there is this one comic on there with a character that totally reminds me of Barbara!" His voice broke into a squeak at the end.

Mal's spine tingled. Last spring she'd drawn a DA robominder who ran the cyborg labor force. She was strict and mean and Mal had based her on Barbara. But no one was ever supposed to know that.

Izzy made a dismissive noise. "No way," she said. "Coincidence."

Marcus shook his head. "For real. It's a robot but it has glasses just like hers and is always yelling at the cyborg kids to keep quiet."

"Did you see that Comic Koala is doing a contest?" Noa asked.

"I know," Marcus moaned. "And we are missing out."

"We keep talking about making one ourselves," Izzy explained to Mal. "I could do the lettering. Marcus and James could totally draw the pictures."

Mal glanced over at the open sketchbook in front of James.

"Wow," she said, leaning forward. He had sketched a superhero but not one she recognized. He wore a mask and had a cape that whipped out behind. Mal imagined James shading in the folds as they rippled in the wind, his large hands holding the pencil delicately. "That's really good, James."

He smiled and lifted his shoulders in a shrug. "Thanks," he said.

"I had the perfect idea for a story," Marcus said, "but you didn't like it."

"A crime-fighting hot dog?" Izzy snorted. "Please."

Noa tilted their head toward Mal. "This happens every time," they whispered. "Everyone gets excited about making a webcomic, and then no one can decide on a story."

Mal smiled, watching Marcus and Izzy throw words back and forth like a Ping-Pong match. "Do you think you'll ever make one?" she asked.

"No," James said. "We can't. You have to be thirteen to post. And none of us is."

"Maybe next year," Noa said, grinning at Marcus, who had stood up and was gesturing wildly as he explained how the hot dog hero would be armed with condiment guns. "Izzy turns thirteen in February. What are the chances they pick a storyline by then?"

James shook his head slowly back and forth. "Slim to none," he said.

"Oh," Noa said, their face lighting up. "Mal, I wanted to ask you something!"

Mal's insides warmed at the glow on Noa's face. "What?" she asked.

"You know I told you about how we're doing a drag holiday story time? Well, here's the best part: I convinced the staff to do a lip sync talent show for it! We are going to have *so* much fun! You'll do a duet with me, right?" They bounced up and down in their seat.

A chill ran through Mal's warm, happy feeling. A duet? In front of people? Mal tried to let the excitement in Noa's face chase away her growing sense of dread. She forced herself to smile back at Noa. "Oh yeah," she said, trying to stall. "When is it?"

"It's the first Saturday in December," Noa said. "I can't wait!"

"Can't wait for what?" asked Marcus. The argument appeared to have ended as quickly as it began.

"The drag holiday story time," Noa said. They linked their

arm through Mal's. "We're doing a duet."

At their touch, a thrill ran up Mal's arm, and she felt a smile bursting across her face. She probably looked ridiculous. At the same time, she wanted to cringe away from the idea of a performance.

"Better you than me," Izzy said to Mal. "I was afraid they'd rope me into performing with them." She lifted her hands dramatically. "*So* not me!"

James nodded in agreement.

"None of them would do it with me," Noa complained. "Even Marcus, who would be great at it!" They glared at him.

Marcus grimaced. "I don't like crowds. Not my thing."

A voice in Mal's head screamed that performing was absolutely not her thing either. But she felt Noa's warm arm hooked through hers and she just wanted to hang on to it. She wanted to give Noa what their other friends couldn't.

"Yeah, I'm into that," Mal said.

The words felt bitter on her tongue, even while Noa responded by dimpling into a smile again. What had she just agreed to? A duet with Noa. At a special event.

"Do you have any song ideas?" Noa asked her, tucking a curl behind their ear.

"I . . ." Mal hesitated, alarm churning in her stomach. Her heart sped up, imagining the crowd of people who would come to a holiday story time.

"Or do you want to look at the costumes first and then

come up with the song?" Noa asked, their eyes gleaming.

Mal wanted to share their excitement but all she felt was panic. She should tell Noa she couldn't do it, but her mouth couldn't figure out how.

"How about we each think of two songs that we like and then next time we can pick the best one?" Noa said. "We only have two weeks and next week is Thanksgiving so we'll need to start practicing really soon." They smiled at Mal. "Let's figure it out Monday?"

"Monday it is," Mal agreed, relieved. Maybe by then she could come up with a way to tell Noa how she felt about crowds.

Mal left the library feeling drained, like she'd just done twenty laps in the pool. At least no one in comic club seemed close to knowing about Dr.BotGirl. But she had somehow agreed to perform in front of a crowd. With Noa.

At home that night, Mal let her brothers eat dinner on the couch and watch TV until just before Mom got home. As soon as the front door opened, Mal went straight up the stairs to her room. She couldn't bring herself to look at math homework or her ELA story. Instead she crashed onto her bed and read manga until Mom came in to shut off the lights. She had no energy for anything else.

COMIC KOALA — USERNAME: DR.BOTGIRL — WEBCOMIC: METAL-PLATED HEART — EPISODE 8, PG 4: LAWS, RIGHTS, AND ROBOTS

Chapter Eleven

MAL HAD TWO FULL DAYS ALL TO HERSELF: Saturday and Sunday. The luxury of lying in bed and doing absolutely nothing felt almost too good to be true. The twins had a birthday party for someone in their class, so Mom had taken them shopping for a gift and then straight there. The house was hers for hours. She slept until almost noon, ate a bowl of Lucky Charms on the couch while watching *My Hero Academia*, and played around on her phone. She completely forgot that she'd planned to hang out with Wendy, until a text popped up on her screen.

Tom (Wendy's bro): Mal, it's Wendy. We still meeting up?

Mal thought about her bed and how part of her wanted to crawl right back under the covers. But she did want to see Wendy. She texted back.

Mal: yeah, where when

Tom (Wendy's bro): Etta's sister has ballet at the rec center at 1 so her mom can drop her off there. maybe pizza pundit? and walk to the thrift emp?

Mal: oh, sure. I didn't know etta was coming

Tom (Wendy's bro): is that ok?

Mal: yep. What time.

Tom (Wendy's bro): in like 30? I gotta go, Tom needs his phone

Mal: Tell your parents you need a phone!

Tom (Wendy's bro): This is Tom now. We tell them every day but Papá won't budge.

Mal: Sorry 😬 Thx for letting her use yours.

Tom (Wendy's bro): No prob.

Mal dropped her phone on the carpet and let her body sink into the couch. Why did it bother her that Etta was coming? Etta was one of her best friends. Etta was great. But something about hanging out with both Wendy and Etta at the same time was so exhausting. They were just so different and Mal never knew who to be around them. Even knowing which pizza to order was harder with both of them.

She squeezed her eyes shut and then heaved her body up into a sitting position. A thrift day with friends was exactly the distraction she needed from her growing mound of overdue homework.

Wendy was sitting on the bench in the courtyard watching a group of boys from school competing over who could climb the highest on the Branch Tree. When Jaydon swung down and landed on the ground, he smiled straight at Wendy for a second. Then he looked away, running a hand self-consciously over his thick, textured curls.

"Aren't you two cute?" Mal teased.

Wendy jumped and turned. Mal was sure Wendy's ears under her blue knit hat were flushed bright red.

"Don't know who you mean," Wendy said, looking pointedly away from the tree.

"Mmhmm," Mal said, crossing her arms. "You and Jaydon were practically making out with your eyes."

"That is gross and untrue." Wendy pulled her thick coat around herself as if the thought of making out gave her chills. "Where is Etta? I'm freezing."

"You're always freezing," Mal said. Then she said teasingly, "I bet Jaydon would warm you up."

Wendy tugged the knit hat down over her eyes and groaned. "Stooooop!"

Mal laughed and sat next to Wendy, throwing an arm

around her. "Okay, okay," she agreed, rubbing Wendy's arm through her coat. "Sorry."

The center doors flew open, and Etta headed toward them, her long skirt flowing out behind her. She wore a tank top and Mal felt Wendy shudder at the sight of her bare, skinny arms ringed with her usual assortment of handmade bracelets.

"How can you stand it?" Wendy asked her as Etta walked up. Etta tilted her head to one side, like a puzzled bird.

"Oh," Etta said, looking at Wendy's coat and hat. She shrugged. "It doesn't feel that cold to me. But . . ." She reached for the tie-dyed sweatshirt knotted around her waist. "If this makes you feel better." Etta slipped the sweatshirt over her head and pulled the hood up to cover her short hair. "Better?"

Wendy nodded. "Thank you, yes. Now can we please go inside?"

The warm air inside the Pizza Pundit smelled like garlic and baking crust. As one the girls took a deep, satisfied breath.

"So good . . ." Wendy sighed.

Behind the counter, Fat Marv slid a fresh pizza onto a cutting board and sliced it into segments. With one practiced motion, he tipped the board and the pizza slid into a waiting box. He tucked the flaps into the sides, closed the box, and called out, "Mr. Darius, I've got yer small Al for ya!" A teenager took the box with a wave and headed outside. Fat Marv was the owner of the Pizza Pundit and he'd been here forever. When Mal first heard someone call him Fat Marv, she'd wanted to stick up for him. But then she saw that his name tag clearly read "Fat Marv" and no one ever called him anything else. If anyone asked, he'd just say, "Ain't nothing wrong with fat." He knew everyone's usual order and everyone's name, though he always called them *mister* or *miss*.

There was a teenager running the register, but Fat Marv still made a point to greet everyone who walked in. He called out, "Miss Mallory, Miss Wendy, Miss Etta, how're you folks doing there?" as they walked up. They waved at him. Etta called out, "Good to see you, Fat Marv! Smells great in here."

"Thank you, Miss Etta, thank you. No Thomas for you today, though, I hate to tell you. We're out of goat cheese."

"Oh." Etta gave a disappointed frown. The Thomas, with pesto and goat cheese, was her favorite.

"We could all share a large Roger instead?" Wendy suggested. "It's the best anyway."

Mal nodded. "Yeah, sure."

"Incorrect," Etta said. "But okay. No meat on my half."

They ordered the Roger: a deep-dish pizza with half cheese and half pepperoni and found a booth by the window. The wall next to them was papered with local announcements and want ads. Wendy saw another Lost Cat flyer tacked over an old summer sale ad. This one looked newer than the one she'd seen on the street, the edges crisp and fresh. Fluffernutter's owner must still be looking for her.

"What are you looking at?" Etta asked her.

"Oh." Mal shrugged. "Just that cat."

Etta turned around in the booth and read the poster. "Oooooh, we should try to find it!"

Wendy looked at Mal and bit her lip nervously. Mal raised her eyebrows and gave her a meaningful nod. They both knew what it meant to get sucked into one of Etta's missions. Unless they wanted to spend the rest of their weekend scouring alleys and knocking on doors, she needed a distraction.

"Oh, hey," Mal said casually. "Look at this one." She pointed to a flyer from the library. "Did you guys know about this? The drag queen story time?"

Etta's eyes lit up, as Mal had known they would. "Oh, no way! That's so fun! We totally should go! Lola would love it." Etta's little sister, Lola, loved dress-up.

"Isn't drag kind of . . . adult?" Wendy asked. Then she looked embarrassed. "I mean, I tried to watch *RuPaul's Drag Race* at home but my parents didn't really like it. They said it was inappropriate."

"Well, drag *can* be inappropriate," Etta said. "But anything can be! It's not like drag is about sex or something. I mean, adult shows might talk about sex, sure, but drag doesn't have to be *about* sex." Etta didn't even try to keep her voice down, and Wendy slid farther down in her seat each time she said the S word.

"Don't talk about s-e-x so loud, Etta!" she hissed.

"I'm not talking *about* sex. I just said that drag *isn't* about sex. I'm actually talking about what's *not* about sex."

Wendy moaned and pulled her knit hat over her eyes.

"Anyway," Mal said loudly, before Wendy could slide entirely under the table, "the drag queen story time is really just a queen dressed up, reading stories to kids."

"That's so cool that the library is doing that," Etta said.

"Yeah, it was basically my friend's idea," Mal said, looking down at her phone. Mentioning Noa to her friends gave her an odd mixture of pride and embarrassment.

"Your friend who?" Wendy asked, sitting up a bit higher in her seat.

"My friend Noa," Mal said, scrolling through posts without really seeing them. "I volunteer with them at the library."

"Noa?" Etta asked, leaning toward Mal. "The enby kid?"

"Enby?" Wendy asked.

"Nonbinary," Etta said.

Wendy frowned. "Binary like the math term?"

"Um, I don't think it's a math thing," Mal said. Granted, she wasn't great at math. "I think binary just means two different categories of something."

"It does," Etta agreed. "So the gender binary says that there are only two kinds of gender: girl or boy."

"Binary math uses two digits," Wendy told them. "So I guess it's similar."

"But the gender binary doesn't work," Etta explained. "Some people are nonbinary. As in, someone who doesn't fit the gender binary of being either a boy or a girl. Enby is another way of saying it. Because of the letters for nonbinary. NB. Get it?"

"Oh, okay," Wendy said. "That makes sense. So your friend Noa isn't a boy or a girl?"

"Right," Mal said. "Noa uses they/them pronouns."

"I know Noa," Etta said. "I didn't know you were friends."

"Yeah," Mal said. "We volunteer together. And we're both helping out with the story time thing."

"Wait, are *you* doing drag?" Etta asked, incredulous.

"No," Mal said quickly. "I mean, we might be dressing up a little but we aren't like, doing the whole . . ." She waved a hand over her face. "Drag thing."

"Still," Etta said, looking at her skeptically. "You are dressing up? Are you performing or something?"

Mal clenched her fingers around her phone. Etta's question hung there, making the air around her feel tight and hot. It pushed her brain to really think about what Noa was planning. Yeah, it was a performance. And she had agreed to do it. She nodded, not meeting her friends' eyes. "It's just a silly thing. Lip sync."

"Mal, don't take this the wrong way," Etta said, "but that doesn't sound like you."

Mal frowned at her phone. She didn't say anything.

"If you want to perform that's great," Wendy said quickly. "I'm impressed. And we'll definitely come support you."

The thought of more people coming to watch her perform a lip sync in a costume made Mal's whole body tense.

"It's just . . ." Wendy trailed off, looking at Etta. Mal saw the look pass between them and hunched over her phone, hoping they would just drop it. Wendy said in a small voice, "Remember the talent show?"

Mal rubbed at her eyes under her glasses. "I remember," she said. It had been a very low-key event at a school assembly at the beginning of the year. Mal had let herself get roped into juggling. It was something she'd learned a couple summers ago at camp, and she'd sometimes juggle clementines at lunch just for fun. But when it was her turn to juggle for the whole middle school, Mal started shaking so hard backstage that she'd barely been able to walk. But she *had* walked—out the back door and straight to the office where she'd called her mom to come pick her up. It didn't take any acting for the nurse to believe she was sick. Just thinking about it now gave her goose bumps.

"Mallory," Etta said, with a look that made Mal want to climb inside Zee's alien robot armor and close the visor. "Wendy and I love you and we know you. And *because* we know you, we would never ask you to get up on a stage."

"Mmhmm," Mal said, turning her eyes to her phone. She could feel herself disconnecting from everything around her.

Etta's laser-green eyes bore into her. "Maybe you should talk to Noa—"

"One large Roger, half pep, half cheese!" Fat Marv called.

"I'll get it!" Mal cried, jumping up from the table. She took her time walking to the counter and back. Things still felt slow around her, like she was drifting in the water. But when she set the pizza in front of them with a "Ta-da!" she felt more grounded. She could stay here, with her friends and this pizza, if they would just not talk about hard things. *Please, just eat*, she wished silently. Etta watched Mal through the steam with those eyes that saw way too much. But Wendy dived for a thick slice of pepperoni deep-dish, and after a moment, Etta grabbed a cheese. Mal relaxed as they enjoyed the greasy goodness of Pizza Pundit. Everything was fine.

Chapter Twelve

MAL SPENT ALL EVENING SATURDAY SKETCHING A
new comic and most of the day Sunday prepping it on her
iPad. She stayed up later than she was supposed to Sunday
night, but Mom didn't even notice. She was folding laundry
downstairs and Mal could hear her laughing at something
on the TV. Mal didn't want to interrupt. She was old
enough to go to bed on her own anyway. Besides, Mom
would have asked about homework. When she finally
uploaded her webcomic and went to bed, Mal fell asleep
immediately.

It was the week of Thanksgiving, and the library was practically empty. Mal stood in the kids' area, staring at the whiteboard. Sometimes Lucy would write a question on there for kids to answer like, "If you could travel anywhere in time and space, when and where would you go?" Mal liked it best when it was a story prompt and then each person would write one more sentence until the story was a long and completely confusing jumble of different ideas and handwriting. It never really made sense but there was something about seeing a story patchworked together by all those different people that Mal liked a lot. Today the board looked like an overzealous kid had decided to erase everything, then gotten distracted. There were only a few words still legible along the bottom: "and eaten alive." Mal scrunched her nose. That was kind of how she felt right now. Like all her overdue homework was coming to take bites out of her all at once. The self-portrait. The ELA story. Math problems. Especially math problems.

"Mal!"

Noa's voice was like a long drink of sunshine. If anything could make her forget about her homework for a while, it was seeing Noa. They were hurrying between the shelves toward Mal, a green velvet cape flowing out behind them.

"Guess what?" they said, their eyes sparkling. "I think

I *might* have convinced Barbara to do a number for the lip sync."

"No!" Mal's jaw dropped. *"Barbara?"*

Noa nodded vigorously, their lopsided curls bobbing up and down over one eyebrow.

Mal looked toward the desk. Light reflected off Barbara's glasses as she pushed them up into her hair and glanced in their direction. Her face was hard to read. Even when her mouth turned up in a smile shape, it looked stiff and fake, like she was following "Instructions for Smiling" step-by-step.

"I'll take your word for it," Mal told Noa.

"Hey, listen, comic club isn't meeting and there are practically no kids here today," Noa said. "And Lucy said we can use her office to practice! Come on!"

Before Mal fully grasped what was happening, Noa had her hand and was pulling her to the back room. The rack of clothes was still in Lucy's office and Noa led her inside. They perched on a stack of boxes and waved in Mal's direction.

"You first," Noa said. "What songs did you think of?"

"Um . . ." Mal felt like sinking into the floor. She sat on Lucy's chair instead. "Well . . . I don't know."

"It's okay. There are no bad ideas! It's a creative process," Noa insisted.

"No, I really don't have any ideas," Mal said. She'd totally forgotten that Noa had asked her to come up with a couple of song choices. What did she know about lip syncs and drag shows? Her biggest concern was how to get out of performing at all.

Noa frowned. "But you did think about it, right?"

"Yes!" Mal insisted, her mind racing. Why was it suddenly so hard to think of a song? "I . . . I just think you probably have much better ideas. And I'm fine with whatever you choose."

Noa didn't look as pleased as she had hoped they would. "Oh, okay," they said. "Well, then . . . My idea was to do a Disney song. Like 'The Circle of Life' or maybe something from *Frozen*."

"Yeah!" Mal nodded. "Great idea." But inside she really hoped Noa wasn't thinking of doing—

"Not 'Let It Go,' don't worry," Noa said, smiling.

Mal laughed. "How did you read my mind? So which one? We need one that two people are in, I guess."

"Yeah," Noa said, pulling out their phone. "Let's look at the lyrics."

Mal searched on her phone too, and they both looked through Disney lyrics together, pointing out ones they thought might work. Mal was reading the lyrics to "Love Is an Open Door" and thinking how perfect it sounded when Noa said, "Oh, maybe this one." They sounded almost shy.

"Which?" she asked.

Noa held up their phone for Mal to see. Mal felt a slow

smile spread over her face and she held up her phone to Noa. They were both looking at the same one: "Love Is an Open Door." Noa's cheek dimpled.

"Well, that's it, then!" They hopped up. "So now we just need to decide if we're going to go realistic or silly. I mean, you could actually dress like Anna if you want to stick to it closely. But personally"—they bit their lip—"I kinda think you rock that snow goddess look. And it's still on theme."

Mal grinned. She pulled the white faux fur from the rack and wrapped it around her shoulders. "Yeah, okay. What about you?"

Noa crossed their arms and stared up at the ceiling for inspiration. "Well . . . if we went with the whole *Frozen* thing, I'd have to be either a gaslighting prince or a goofy reindeer guy. I mean, the latter is better, obvi, but I think I want to do my own thing." They stepped to the rack of clothes and started looking through them. "What should I wear?" they mused aloud.

"Glitzy pageant queen?" Mal asked, pointing to the red sequined dress.

"Or . . ." Noa held out a tutu. "Tangerine ballerina?"

Mal shrugged.

"You're right," Noa said. "Too boring. Ooooohhh!" They sucked in their breath dramatically. "I know! How about I also wear roller skates? And wings."

Mal giggled. "So, is our whole vibe just complete

randomness? Like, I could also wear cat ears?"

Noa's eyes gleamed. "Yes! You don't know how to hula-hoop, do you, by chance? Or juggle?"

"Um, I do, actually," Mal said. "Juggle."

"Wait, for real? I was totally kidding!" Noa looked absolutely delighted. "You juggle? That is amazing!"

Before Mal could respond, they heard a raised voice from the next office over.

"—can't be serious!" The voice sounded tinny, like it was coming through a speaker phone. And angry.

Noa and Mal locked eyes and without saying a word they both stepped closer to the open door. The voice continued speaking, rising in pitch. "I honestly thought I had heard wrong. Not at our library, that's what I said!"

The calm voice of the library manager, Zachary, answered her. "Ma'am, our library hosts a variety of programs. The drag story time—" But the woman on the phone interrupted.

"This is not something I want my children exposed to! If you are going to willfully indoctrinate our babies with pornog—" Her voice cut off. Zachary must have turned off the speaker phone. Mal heard the sound of someone walking closer, and then Zachary's office door shut. He answered the woman on the phone, but his voice was muffled now and Mal couldn't make out the words. She looked at Noa. Their black-rimmed eyes were huge and worried.

"That was about the drag queen story time, wasn't it?" Mal asked.

Noa nodded. "It has to be." They plopped into Lucy's chair and chewed a fingernail.

Mal sank down, crossing her legs to sit on the floor. "She sounded really mad," Mal said slowly.

"Yeah."

"Do you think Zachary would cancel it?" Mal asked.

"I doubt it," Noa said, but they looked worried. "There were some people who got mad about the Pride story time in June, and they didn't cancel it. They did get extra security, though."

Mal shivered. Extra security? Did that mean they thought people would get violent? Fighting was one of the things that made Mal's skin crawl, like Coach Perkins's voice or Etta yelling. Fighting was something Mal did her absolute best to avoid, always.

"Maybe if people are that upset, they should think about canceling it," Mal said. Noa looked up, their gray-blue eyes startled. "Just for safety," Mal clarified. "If people are really angry . . ." She trailed off. Why was Noa looking at her like that?

"You think Zachary should give in?" Noa said.

"No," Mal said, her heart beating faster. "Not give in. I just mean . . . I just think it would be safer." She bit her lip, imagining someone threatening Lucy or Shuga Toast. Or Noa. "Maybe," she whispered, looking at the floor. This wasn't coming out how she meant it at all.

"They are bullies, Mal," Noa said. "Bullies who think people they don't understand are wrong!"

Their voice shook on the last word, and Mal looked up. Noa's eyes, those remarkable eyes, were filled with tears.

"They think *I'm* wrong," Noa whispered.

Mal's heart stuttered. But before she could say anything, Noa jumped up and ran out of the office.

"Noa, wait!" Mal called after them. She started out the door, then remembered the fur she was wearing and scrambled to remove it. She threw it over the top of the rack and rushed out. Mal scanned the nearly empty library for Noa's green velvet cape. She spun in a circle. She wanted to yell at the top of her lungs, *"Noa, come back! They're wrong, not you!"* Noa was nowhere in sight.

"Looking for your friend?"

Mal whirled and came face-to-face with Barbara. She was pushing a cart full of books and peering over her glasses at Mal. Not trusting herself to speak, Mal only nodded.

"I'm afraid they're gone." Barbara pointed her chin toward the front door. "Didn't seem eager to stick around." She quirked one gray eyebrow at Mal.

Mal felt her breath coming in short, angry puffs. Barbara

the Brutal didn't know anything. Barbara the Brutal didn't know what Noa was angry about. It wasn't Mal. It was the woman on the phone and the other people who didn't understand. Not Mal.

But Noa hadn't run out after hearing the woman on the phone, Mal thought, her heart sinking. They'd run out after what Mal said to them. Tears prickled at Mal's eyes. If Barbara was judging her right now, maybe she was right.

On Tuesday, a gloomy cloud followed Mal from class to class. It clung to her during ELA while she tried to scratch out a story idea for Mr. Emerson that wasn't *Metal-Plated Heart*. It pulled her down into darkness all through math, which she had basically stopped even trying to follow, and through art. Miss Hill was checking on their self-portraits. They were due before Thanksgiving break, which started tomorrow afternoon. All Mal had so far was a vague outline and the list of adjectives she was supposed to use.

Wendy's self-portrait, a drawing she had traced from an actual picture of herself, had planets in the background, orbiting around her. She was almost done, and Mal watched her pasting strips of paper with the descriptive words printed on them along the lines of the planets' orbits. Even though she wasn't much of an artist, Wendy's portrait was neat and careful, just like her.

Yasmin had brought fabric from home to make the head covering on her self-portrait. The peach-colored cloth formed a hijab around her pencil-sketched face, the folds falling gracefully over her shoulders. Yasmin had framed it with family pictures, magazine photos of plants, and a drawing of her hot-pink roller skates. Right now Yasmin was writing her descriptive words across the bottom of the portrait in both English and Arabic, her pretty face knitted in concentration.

Mal looked back at her half-done portrait, wrinkled and covered with eraser marks. Every time she tried to sketch something, she found herself drawing Zee instead or copying from someone next to her and she had to erase it. It wasn't that she hadn't had ideas. But whenever she thought of something, her brain would second-guess it and argue against it until she finally gave up.

"Mallory," Miss Hill said quietly, "every time I see some progression you seem to end up back at the beginning. Can you tell me what's going on?"

Mallory wanted to answer Miss Hill. But everything felt fuzzy in her mind. She didn't know why she couldn't do this. Every time she tried to give some kind of shape to her portrait, it felt wrong.

Miss Hill laid a warm hand on Mal's arm. "Even the most creative minds have blocks sometimes. Why don't I give you an extension? Take it home with you over break. Look

135

over the words your classmates used to describe you. Maybe something will inspire you."

Wyatt was even louder than usual that evening. Winston had three meltdowns before dinner. And Mal zoned out while boiling the water for mac and cheese. It overflowed all over the burner, putting out the flame and splashing her arm. She stuck her arm in the sink and ran cold water over it, sleeve and all, grateful it hadn't hit her bare skin. In the only good thing that happened all day, Mom came home a bit early. She checked on Mal's arm and told her to go change her shirt while she finished making dinner. Mal changed straight into her pajamas and probably would have gone right to bed if she hadn't been so hungry. The smell of Mom's mac and cheese, somehow better than it ever was when Mal made it, drew her back downstairs.

Around a spoonful of food, Mal asked, "So, we'll be at Dad's until Sunday?"

"Please don't talk with your mouth full, Mallory."

Mal swallowed. "Sorry. So, we're going to Dad's tomorrow until Sunday?"

Mom nodded. "Yes, so make sure to take any homework you have with you. And you'll be at Grandma's for part of that time, so you may as well take your homework there too." She looked at Mal conspiratorially. "It'll give you an excuse to escape if you need it."

Mal was the oldest of the cousins, so she usually got stuck either playing with the younger kids or sitting around while the grown-ups talked. But either of those would be better than working on math or her self-portrait.

"And you'll be at Daddy's?" Winston asked.

Mom's mouth tightened the tiniest bit. "No, sweetie."

"Where will you be?" Winston asked.

"Just for the turkey, though!" Wyatt yelled, spraying a bit of mac and cheese onto the table. "You will come just for the turkey!"

"Don't talk with your mouth full, honey," Mom said. "And remember, Mommy isn't going to be there for Thanksgiving this year. But you will be at Grandma's, just like always. With Daddy and Grandma and Uncle Todd and Auntie Marie."

"And Becca and Minnie and Archie," Winston added.

"And Archie!" Wyatt repeated. Of all their relatives, Archie, their Grandma's Havanese, was unquestionably the twins' favorite. No one could compete with an adorable, floppy-eared lapdog.

Mom hadn't answered Winston's question, and it nagged at Mal. If Mom was just going to stay home, why wouldn't she say so?

"Are you going somewhere?" Mal asked.

Mom busied herself brushing invisible crumbs off the table into her hand and emptying them onto her napkin. Mal waited.

"I . . . am—" Mom said. She looked up. "I'm going to Sacramento."

Mal felt her insides twist. The boys cried out in indignation, and Mom raised her voice. "It's just for a few days," she insisted. "I'll be back on Sunday when you get home."

"*I* want to visit Halmoni!" Winston said.

"Me too!" Wyatt yelled.

"I know," Mom said in a soothing voice. "And we will all go visit soon. But for right now, I need to go on my own." She lifted her chin a fraction as she spoke, and that small movement felt to Mal like someone putting on armor. A picture of her mom wearing Comic Koala's mech helmet flashed in her brain. Mal wanted to laugh and cry all at once.

"You will be just fine while I'm gone," Mom was saying. "And you'll get to spend time with your dad. My office is closed too, so this seemed like the best time." Mom met Mal's eyes, her expression expectant. Mal knew that Mom wanted her to understand.

"When will *we* get to go?" Wyatt demanded.

"How about for Seollal?" Mom said, tapping his nose. "That's your favorite holiday anyway."

Seollal, the Korean lunar new year, was much more fun to celebrate with their Korean relatives. And getting out of Ohio in February was always a good idea, Mal told herself.

"But Seollal is *years* away," Winston said, his lip jutting out.

Mal took a breath, trying to lift her chin like Mom had. "Seollal's only a few months away," Mal told her brothers. "It'll be here before you know it."

"That's right!" Her mom beamed at her. "We will all get to visit with Halmoni and everyone else then."

Mal smiled back, doing her best to look supportive. Mom probably did need to get away. She hadn't seen her family in Sacramento since before the divorce. But the words Mal had overheard the other night haunted the back of her brain. What if Halmoni and Emo Sue tried to get Mom to move there? What if that's what Mom's trip was all about?

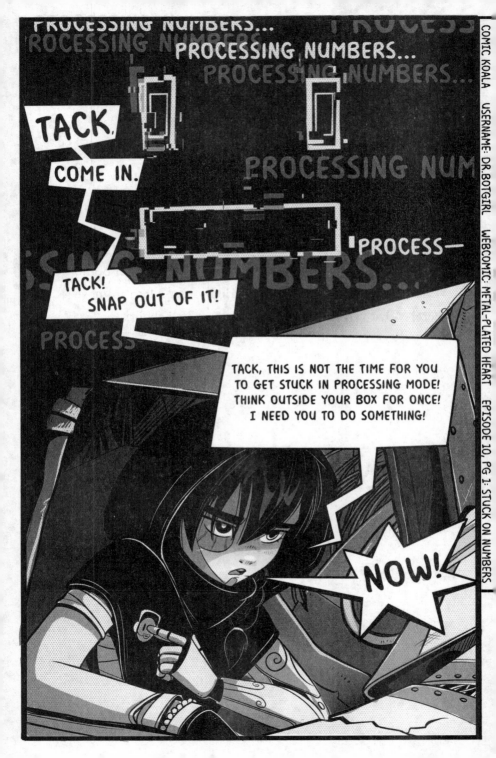

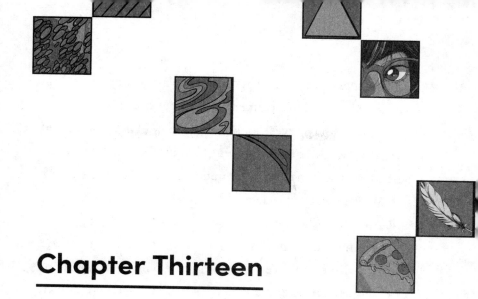

Chapter Thirteen

"SO YOU'LL SIGN, RIGHT?"

Mal blinked up at Etta. Apparently nodding and agreeing could get her only so far. "Sign?" Mal asked slowly.

Etta looked at Mal and Wendy, her green eyes widening in exasperation. She was sitting across from them at lunch, but she'd set down her sandwich a while ago and forgotten about it. Etta ran her fingers through her hair. It stuck out from her head like spiky cotton candy.

"The petition! Were either of you listening?!" Etta's voice went up a notch.

She'd been talking about housing again and how bad the

homelessness problem in Columbus was getting. But Mal had tuned out before she mentioned a petition.

Wendy's dark eyes looked worried. "Etta," she said carefully, "we *have* been listening. I'm just not sure that's the best idea. You can't bring a bunch of random adults into a school, even on the weekend."

Uh-oh, Mal thought.

Etta's mouth hardened into a stubborn line. "They have nowhere else to go, Wendy! Our gym would totally work as an emergency weekend shelter. It's just sitting there empty, and people are on the streets!"

At the next table over some kids looked up at Etta's outburst. Mal saw Wendy meet Jaydon's eyes and then look down at her lunch tray, her ears turning pink.

"People do use the school on the weekends, though," Wendy said, keeping her voice low. "They use it for basketball. And extracurriculars and stuff."

"And sports are more important than people's lives?" Etta said, her voice still too loud. Everyone around them was looking now, and Mal flashed them all a bright "everything's fine" smile before leaning toward Etta.

"That's not what she's saying, Etta," Mal said soothingly. "You know that's not what she means."

"Then why do we get to have sports while people are going to be sleeping on the streets during winter?" Etta's voice cracked, and she glared down at her sandwich. Angry tears glinted in her eyes.

Wendy bit her lip. "Obviously, I agree with you that it's not fair. But you have to be logical about it, Etta. Ms. Whitman will never approve of bringing unknown adults into a school building. Just stop and think it through before you—"

"That's why nothing ever happens," Etta snapped. "Because *logical* people get stuck processing information and never actually *do* anything!"

She stood up, suddenly, as if she'd been jerked by a string. "I gotta go," she said, grabbing her tray. She rushed out of the cafeteria, like a small pink whirlwind. Wendy bowed her head and started folding the foil lid of her applesauce into a neat square.

"She didn't mean it," Mal assured her.

"Isn't that what I do?" Wendy said, her voice small. "Get stuck?"

"No," Mal insisted, putting a hand on Wendy's arm. "Not at all. Besides, being logical is a good thing. She was just upset."

Wendy gave her a half smile. "Thanks, Mal."

Mallory couldn't help feeling relieved that Etta wasn't in her next class. When Etta got angry about something, even for good reason, it always made Mal's stomach twist. Especially when it was something Etta couldn't let go.

Apparently, this was one of those ideas.

"Did you hear about Etta?" K.K. asked as they got ready

for early dismissal. "She got sent to Ms. Whitman's office."

"For what?" Mal asked.

"Disrupting science class," Wendy said. "She was still worked up from lunch. She was all jittery and couldn't pay attention when she was called on."

"So Ms. Park finally yelled at her," K.K. said. "And then Etta yelled back."

"She yelled at the teacher?" Mal asked. That was a lot even for Etta.

"I mean she was more just yelling at the world," Wendy explained. "She said, 'How am I supposed to care about the scientific method when people don't have homes!'"

"Ms. Park did not know how to handle it," K.K. said, shaking her head. "When she told her to go see Ms. Whitman, Etta just yelled back, 'Good, I need to talk to her anyway,' and stomped out."

Mal was supremely grateful she wasn't in their science class. Just the thought of that much yelling made her feel sick. "That's Etta for you," she said weakly.

Wendy nodded. "Full speed ahead."

"Full speed ahead," Mal agreed. It was the phrase they used whenever Etta went off on one of her campaigns.

"Oh!" K.K. said suddenly. "Full speed ahead!" She scrambled for her phone and started typing something.

Mal and Wendy looked at each other curiously. "What's up?" Mal asked.

"That's exactly what it said in that robot drawing," K.K. said. "You know that boy James? He's a really good artist and he's been helping me make some posters for student council. Anyway, he showed me this comic. . . . Hang on."

A chill crept slowly down Mal's spine.

"Look at this." K.K. held out her phone. It was Mal's webcomic. Smoker, the robot Zee accidently built with a faulty personality chip, was billowing smoke from her bright pink sides and wheeling in circles. The word bubble under it said, "Full speed ahead!" The chill on Mal's spine turned to solid ice.

Wendy let out a soft laugh. "That robot does remind me of Etta," she said.

"But it's not," Mal said, too quickly. "It's not her."

"I know," Wendy said, looking at Mal curiously. "I mean, it's a robot."

"Except James thinks this could actually be based on real people," K.K. said, scrolling through the webcomic. "He showed me one episode that is seriously eerie." She held out the screen and Wendy and Mal leaned in. "Tell me who this reminds you of."

It was the episode where the evil alien runs for president and charms everyone. A girl in the crowd is blowing him kisses. Mal had drawn her with heart eyes and a strand of blond hair twisted around her finger.

"Um," Wendy hesitated.

K.K. said, "I'll give you a hint. The alien she's in love with runs for president, but then everyone finds out he's actually horrible."

Wendy stared at K.K. "Seriously? Is it about Brett?" She looked closer at the comic girl. "That's Fiona!"

"Right?" K.K. said. "It has to be."

Mal's stomach sank. She licked her lips and forced a laugh. "I don't think so. The . . . hair . . . is too curly." It was a weak argument and they both ignored her.

"'*Metal-Plated Heart*,'" Wendy read out loud. "I'm going to look that up. You really think it's about people from LPA?"

K.K. shrugged. "I only saw a few episodes. But James said his friend has read them all and he's positive whoever made them goes here," she said, pocketing her phone.

Mal forced herself to take a slow, calming breath. But inside, she could feel a deep, dark cave yawning open.

Mal had lived in the same house her entire life. That meant she had twelve years' worth of crafts, drawings, posters, books, trinkets, and pictures that made her bedroom her own space. Lots of those had been given to her, at birthdays or Christmases. Some were things she had made herself. She had never had to think about any of it. She had just lived one day at a time and little by little she had accumulated a room full of stuff that felt like her. Then her dad had moved into his apartment six months ago, and all of a sudden there was a brand-new bedroom that Mal was supposed to live in every other weekend.

The boys had immediately given Dad a whole list of things they wanted. They had matching Avengers comforters, wall lamps shaped like Stormtrooper helmets, and a growing collection of sticks, feathers, and special stones in a little drawer.

The only thing in Mal's room that felt like hers was her quilt. Grandma, Dad's mom, had made the quilt for Mal when she was born, and Mal brought that with her from home every time she came here. She felt a guilty pang at that word: "home." She should probably call it "Mom's house," at least around Dad. But it was still home to her. And this room wasn't. Dad had offered to buy her new sheets, posters, and lamps. But Mal couldn't really decide on anything. The room was still nearly as bare as when he had first moved in. It made her feel almost as if she were traveling. Like this room was just an Airbnb.

After dinner on Wednesday, Mal told Dad she had homework and left him to hang out with the twins. It seemed like it should be his turn, she thought, feeling a flicker of resentment. She felt bad almost immediately. It wasn't his fault his work schedule kept him busy most days after school.

Miss Hill had given Mal a thick cardboard envelope to carry her self-portrait in and she set it on the dresser of her empty, still-unfamiliar room. She slid the picture out. It was the good heavy kind of drawing paper, but she had erased her attempts at outlining her face so many times that it was worn and wrinkled. What had Miss Hill told her? Look through the adjectives and see if they brought inspiration? Mal dug into her bag and pulled out the crumpled paper with her cartoon sketch of Noa on the back. She smoothed it out flat and looked at the list of descriptive words. Some of these were the basic words kids wrote for anyone they didn't know too well: *Nice, friendly, smart.* But someone had described her as logical, which surprised her a bit. Someone else had described her as sensitive. Also quiet. And an extrovert. Those were completely contradictory. And how could she be both "thoughtful" *and* "impulsive"? Mal frowned. Her classmates thought she was "shy" but also "outgoing"? That made no sense. Which one was it? Mal hated projects like this. How was she supposed to use these words to figure out who she was? She shoved the list and the portrait back into the envelope.

Mal flopped onto her bed, pulled her quilt up to her chin, and stared at the blank walls. She could hear the boys downstairs and her dad playing classical music in the kitchen. She imagined Mom in Sacramento, chatting with her sister. Maybe they were cooking Japchae or rice cakes with Halmoni. Unless her mom was out interviewing for jobs. Mal shivered under her quilt. Was Mom looking at apartments? Had Mom already found them new schools? Her eyes burned.

That night, Mal dreamed she stood in front of a classroom full of kids she didn't know. They pointed to a table covered with sticky name tags and told her to put one on. But the name tags all had different adjectives written on them and each time Mal reached for one it rolled up and turned into a rice cake. She woke up grumpy and hungry on Thanksgiving morning.

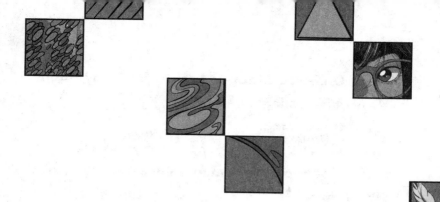

Chapter Fourteen

ETTA WAS ONE OF THE ONLY KIDS IN SCHOOL WHO didn't have social media. But she did have a flip phone that got text messages.

Mal: Hi, Etta

Etta: Hi

Mal: Happy Thanksgiving

Etta: You know that this is considered a Day of Mourning right?

Mal: It is?

Etta: I mean for the Wampanoag people it's definitely not a celebration.

Mal: Oh, so . . . what do I say? I can't say Happy Day of Mourning

Etta: Never mind.

Mal: Are you okay? I heard about yesterday.

Etta: Not really. Whitman said we couldn't use the school as a shelter, no matter how many signatures my petition got.

Mal: sorry

Etta: The world is just so unfair sometimes. And nothing I do changes anything.

Mal: Whoa, not true. You do so much! You are always doing stuff!

Etta: But it's not enough.

Mal: You can't fix everything Etta. Just focus on what you can.

Etta: Yeah. Like apologizing to Wendy? 😬

Mal: Probably. But hey, you are a force for good. Remember that!

Etta: Thanks, Mal.

Mal: Do you have Noa's number?

Etta: I think so.

Mal: Can you ask them to text me?

Etta: done.

Mal: thanks, FFG

Etta: ??

Mal: Force For Good

Etta: ha. Thx Mal.

Also, here's a video about the Wampanoag people. You know, the native people from that whole 1st Thanksgiving myth? If you want to know more.

Mal: OK, thanks.

Mallory's mood was gloomy as she grabbed her quilt and her duffel bag of things for their overnight stay at Grandma's and headed downstairs Thursday morning. The boys were having some kind of competition to see who could stuff more toys in their backpacks while Dad cleaned up breakfast.

If Mom were here, she'd be cooking something to take to Grandma's. Like Brussels sprouts with kimchi or soy-glazed sweet potatoes. There wouldn't be anything like that this year. Mal wondered what Dad was bringing. What if he had forgotten completely? Without Mom to remind him, Dad seemed to forget about normal things like meals all the time.

He hadn't forgotten today. His plan, as he explained to Mal in the car, was to pick up potato salad from the grocery store on the way to Grandma's.

"My phone reminded me," he told her. "I put things in the reminder app and it tells me when I need to do them! I can even tell it to remind me of something when I'm leaving the house or when I get in the car."

"That's great, Dad," Mal said. She felt a lump in her

throat, and she swallowed hard. He was so proud of himself. Over the stupid reminder app. Mal's skin felt prickly, and she pulled her hood over her head and turned toward the window. She wasn't in the mood to talk about apps that were replacing Mom in his life.

Mal woke up an hour later as they were pulling into Grandma's driveway. She was still blinking sleep from her eyes as the boys burst from the car to the house in a whirlwind of energy. She followed more slowly, waiting for Grandma to catch each of the twins in a hug before they ran off in search of Archie.

"Get over here, Cupcake," Grandma said, opening her arms wide. Mal felt her grandmother's hug envelop her, prickly edges and all. Mal held on to her for longer than normal. "There, there," she murmured into Mallory's ear. Grandma didn't pull away until Mal finally let go, wiping the corner of her eye. Her grandma's face crinkled into a smile. "Come on inside, my dear. Everything will be all right."

And it was, at first. Mal wasn't sure what she had expected. Maybe for Aunt Marie to ask Mal how she was feeling about the divorce in her syrupy-sweet voice. But Grandma kept everyone busy with meal prep. Mal helped stir the cranberry sauce, listening to the conversation flit by. Little Becca lost both her front teeth the day before school pictures. Archie's new groomer had put bows on his ears. It was unseasonably rainy. Then the turkey was in the oven and the grown-ups settled into the living room to watch reruns of the Macy's parade. Dad passed out coffee and told the story he told every Thanksgiving, about the time Uncle Todd tried to deep-fry a turkey. The twins and their little cousins found Grandma's basket of toys and puzzles. Mal had been tasked with peeling apples for the pie and she set up where she could see the TV. On the screen a group of people danced to a song from some Broadway show. The dancing couples were lip-syncing, which made her think of Noa. A girl in a cute purple dress with ruffles twirled around her date in a suit. Then the camera showed a close-up of the couple, and Mal realized they were both girls. The peeler in her hand froze, and she shot a quick glance around to see if anyone else noticed. Dad glanced at the screen, then turned back to his conversation. But Aunt Marie had stopped folding napkins to watch.

A crowd of people danced over a giant star that said, "Macy's Thanksgiving Day Parade," and the main couple started to slow dance. The way they each stared at each other, with huge smiles on their faces as if looking into the other girl's eyes was all they ever wanted to do, made a thrill run down Mal's back. She wondered if that was how she looked when she smiled at Noa. And then the girl in the suit reached her hand out and touched the other girl's face, and they stepped toward each other, like magnets, drawn together in the middle of the crowd, and kissed. Mal froze. Her body felt tingly and light. The girls on the screen pulled apart and lifted their clasped hands in one coordinated motion along with all the other dancers as the song ended in applause.

Mal heard an intake of breath and then Aunt Marie said, "Well, that was completely unnecessary."

She turned to look at her aunt, hoping she was talking about something else. But no. Aunt Marie was staring at the TV, her mouth pursed in a frown. The announcers came back on, talking about the performance. It was from a Broadway show about two girls who weren't allowed to go to their high school prom together. Mal looked at Dad, but he was looking down at his phone. Uncle Todd had turned around when Aunt Marie spoke and was listening to the TV now.

"Doesn't surprise me," Uncle Todd said. "Can't get away from political agendas even on Thanksgiving." He shook his head in disgust and sipped his coffee.

"It's not an agenda," Mal said. Her voice sounded way too loud. She suddenly felt as if everyone in the room was staring at her. "It's just two people who love each other."

Aunt Marie blinked. "It's not that I am against that," she said tightly. "But there is a time and place. There could have been a warning at least." Her eyes flew to where her girls were playing with the twins. Neither of them was paying any attention. And even if they were, thought Mal, what did it matter? What did Aunt Marie think would happen if her daughters saw two girls kiss? And if her aunt and uncle had a problem with that, what would they think about someone like Noa?

Mal opened her mouth again, but Dad's eyes locked on to hers. He shook his head no, just slightly. Mal snapped her mouth closed, her eyes drilling into his. Dad hated confrontation, she knew that. She had never heard him call out his sister on anything. But maybe now he would. Maybe he wanted Mal to stay quiet because he was going to handle it. He'd tell Aunt Marie that there was nothing inappropriate about two girls kissing. He'd make sure they knew where the Marshes stood. That's what Mom would do.

"Mal, why don't you go help Grandma in the kitchen?" Dad said.

She stared at him. A wild wind blew through the deep cave inside her. He gave her a smile, that grown-up kind that was supposed to be encouraging. Mal could almost hear him thinking, *Don't rock the boat.* But all he said was, "She's probably ready for those apples now."

Mal stood, so quickly she felt light-headed, and carried the bowl of apples toward the kitchen. Behind her, she heard her dad say something about the football game, and Uncle Todd responded. The conversation was back on safe ground. Mal's breathing sped up. She pushed through the swinging door into the kitchen.

Grandma looked up from the flat sheet of piecrust she was rolling and smiled at Mal. "Well, hello there, Cupcake. You ready to put this pie together?" The smile faded as she saw Mal's face. Mal put the bowl of apples on the counter with a hard clunk. The word "unnecessary" echoed in her head.

"Cupcake," Grandma said, setting down the rolling pin and opening her arms wide. "You need some sugar?"

Grandma's apron was covered with flour, but Mal leaned right into her, feeling Grandma's arms wrap around her as the tears came. She sobbed, her body shaking, and thought of her aunt's tight mouth and her uncle's words. And her dad, going along with whatever everyone else said. Always so quick to agree, as long as that made everyone happy. And they were happy. Everyone else was fine. They were back to chatting about football and watching the parade. Only Mal was making such a big deal over nothing. *Unnecessary.*

"There, there," Grandma murmured, rubbing her back. "Tell Grandma everything."

Mal choked out a long string of words that made no sense at all. Mom would have said something if she were here and the girls just wanted to dance together and that shouldn't need a warning and why was Dad too scared of his own sister to say so and also girls kissing *was* necessary, actually. She paused to take a shaky breath and wipe her eyes.

Grandma led her to a chair and handed her a tissue. She waited while Mal blew her nose and wiped her face and took another shuddering breath.

"Now, Cupcake," Grandma said, with a brisk nod of her

head. "I don't know exactly what happened, but I know something my daughter said hurt you. And sounds like some things my son *didn't* say hurt you even more." She raised her eyebrows in a question and Mal nodded slowly. "He's never been one for speaking his mind. Or knowing his mind either, if I'm laying it all out in the open." Grandma shook her head thoughtfully.

Mal said in a small voice, "I'm just like him, aren't I?"

Grandma lifted her eyebrows. "Do you know your mind?"

Mal hesitated, then said, "About this? Yes."

Grandma nodded, her eyes fixed on Mal's. "Well, now. That's the first step. The speaking-your-mind part, that's a trickier bit, but it's a whole lot easier once you know your mind."

"But I left. Dad told me to leave so . . . I just left. I should have argued with them. Or something." Mal felt tears welling up in her eyes again.

"What do you wish you had said?"

Mal thought. "Well, I guess . . . I did say something."

"Oh?"

"Uncle Todd said that girls kissing was a political thing. An agenda. And I said no; it's just two people who love each other."

Understanding dawned on Grandma's face. "Ahhhh . . . ," she said. "Is that what this is all about?" Then she looked toward the living room. "I've half an inclination to go in there and give them a piece of my mind. A mind which I know well. And I've got years of practice in speaking it." There was a glint in her eyes that made Mal think she meant it. But then she caught the look on Mal's face, and she softened. "Well, I suppose that can wait for now, but I'll be pulling my Marie and her husband aside for a chat before the day's out. This is my house after all, and I still get to tell them how to behave in it."

Grandma tilted her head to the side and gave Mal a look. There was a smudge of flour on one cheek and her eyes crinkled at the corners.

"Sounds to me like you said just the right thing. Is there anything else you want to say? Anything you want to tell me, Cupcake?"

Mal chewed her bottom lip.

"I'm not sure. I . . ." She trailed off.

"Whatever you want to say, you know you can tell me. You know I love you for who you are."

"But that's just it. That's the problem!" Mal's breath sped up again. "I'm not sure *who* I am. I know you're asking me if . . . if I want to come out. As gay. I mean, lesbian or whatever the right label is but . . . I just don't know. None of that feels right." She looked down, embarrassed. But that rushing wind inside that had started when her dad sent her out of the room was still there, pushing the words out. "I just don't want to be fake! What if I say I'm queer and then I decide I'm really straight?"

"Could be that you're bisexual," Grandma mused.

Mal looked at her in surprise. She didn't even know her grandmother knew the word "bisexual."

"You mean that I like both boys and girls?"

Grandma lifted her shoulders. "Could be," she said.

Mal thought about that. Sure, maybe bisexual felt more right than anything else. She'd liked both boys and girls before. But why did her likes have to be on two sides like that? Why did her likes have to go in a box at all?

"Why do I have to be anything?" Mal asked. "Why do I need a label when none of them feels right? It's easier to just be nothing."

"You aren't nothing, Cupcake. Don't you ever let yourself believe that. Your somebodyness is one of the most valuable things you have. Hang on to that. You are somebody. You are my Mallory."

Tears stung Mal's eyes. "You asked if I know my mind but I don't! I mean, I know it's definitely okay for girls to kiss, but I don't know if *I* would want to. Sometimes, yeah, I've wanted that, but then other times I don't." Mal felt hot, like she was feverish or exercising, which was *so* not her thing. "I feel like I'm never one thing. I'm just all kinds of things stitched together or worse, different things every day. Like there is no real *me*, just a mixture of other people around me."

"Hey now," Grandma said, taking Mal's hands in her own

soft ones. "Mallory Marsh is more than a patchwork of other people. You are the toddler who swam before she could run. You're the sister who can always tell the difference between her brothers when even I can't sometimes. You see the good in everyone around you and you always know how to smooth things over. And you are smart as a whip too."

Mal made a dismissive sound, but Grandma held up a finger. "That memory of yours is a wonder. Tell me you don't have a whole treasure vault of movies you could probably quote word for word?" Mal shrugged and nodded. "Now, I don't understand half of these shows of yours," Grandma said, waving a hand toward the hook in the corner where Mal's denim jacket hung, covered in patches. "But all those things mean something to you. This is *you* and no one else. Whether you are L.G.B.T.Q.I.A."—she spoke the letters slowly, as if she were reading them out loud— "or some other letter entirely. You still have pieces of you that are Mallory, loud and clear."

Mal sniffed. She thought of all the patches she'd chosen and added to her jacket. She remembered arguments in comic club and how she was the only one who loved *Nausicaä* best of all. Maybe she didn't completely hide who she was around others.

Grandma dusted flour from her hands. "And do *not* repeat this on pain of losing dessert privileges, but of all my grandkids, you give the best hugs." She opened her arms, and

Mal gave her grandma another hug.

"Thanks, Gran-Gran," she said, her face pressed into Grandma's shoulder. She smelled like cinnamon. Mal pulled away and smiled at her.

"Also, how are you so cool?"

Grandma laughed and brushed some flour off Mal's sleeve. "Old people don't have to be close-minded, you know."

"Yeah," Mal elbowed her playfully. "Look at you talking about 'bisexual' and LGBTQIA. How do you even know about this stuff? TikTok?"

"Goodness, no." She held up her hands. "That app is too loud for me. But Archie's new groomer is a very nice young . . . person. Who has explained a few things to me."

"Person?"

Grandma's brow furrowed a bit as if she were concentrating on each word. "They identify as nonbinary," she said carefully.

"Archie's groomer is enby?" Mal asked.

Grandma frowned. "I believe you have lost me." She stood up. "Thank goodness that I don't need all the right words to love someone." She patted Mal's arm. "Now, why don't you help me fill this pie?"

Later that night, Mal sat cross-legged on her usual bed at Grandma's house. The list of adjectives from her class and her blank self-portrait lay on her quilt in front of her. She tapped her pencil thoughtfully against her chin, then drew an outline. Shaggy, shoulder-length hair; bangs that hung too long over the tops of her glasses; slightly stooped shoulders. The lines were so basic, so boring. She was nothing but pencil sketches over eraser lines on wrinkled paper. Mal sighed.

Her phone buzzed, and Mal dropped her pencil. She scooped up her phone and looked at the screen.

Unknown number: Hi, Mal.

Etta gave me your number.

Mal's heart skipped a beat. *Noa?* she typed.

Noa: Yeah

Mal: Noa, I'm SO SORRY

Noa: No, it's ok

Mal: Those people are totally wrong and we are going to do the story time. They can't bully us out of it.

Noa: Thanks Mal. I'm sorry I ran out like that. I was more upset at them not you

But it wasn't fair. Sorry

Mal: No I'm sorry! I shouldn't have said any of that. I just wanted to protect you

Noa: protect me?

Mal: I just thought you might be safer if there wasn't a drag show but . . . I shouldn't have said that.

Noa: I mean, I get that. The safety thing. but

I don't think the solution is for people like me to go

away, you know?

Mal: No! I don't want you to go away!

Noa: I know, I know. But that's kind of the easy solution for stuff like this.

Mal: What do you mean?

Noa: When people get uncomfortable around people like me it's usually because they just don't know anything about it. But explaining it is hard. It's easier for them if we just . . . shut up and hide.

Mal stared at her phone. She thought about all the times she had pushed away something she thought or something she wanted because it was easier to just go along with things. She wanted everyone around her to be comfortable and happy, even if that meant some part of herself stayed hidden. Is that what she had done to Noa when she said they should think about canceling the story time? Her heart clenched as she messaged back.

Mal: Is that what you thought I wanted?

Noa: I don't know

Mal: I don't at all!!! I was worried about you bc I DON'T want you to disappear. Not ever. I want you to show up and be your usual, incredible self.
If that makes anyone uncomfortable, THEY can hide, not you!

Noa: Yeah?

Mal: Definitely

Noa: Thanks Mal. That means a lot.

Mal: Yeah, I've got your back

Noa: So . . . how's your Thanksgiving?

Mal: Um . . . I shouldn't say Happy Thanksgiving, right?

Noa: As a firm supporter of indigenous people I'm gonna say no

Mal: Did Etta send you that video too?

Noa: Yeah. It is really interesting actually. I didn't know about the day of mourning thing.

Mal: OK, I'll watch it later.
And it's going fine. We're at my grandma's. She's pretty cool.

Noa: Nice. We're at my uncle's. And the cousins are calling me, so got to go

Mal: Back into the fray, huh? Sorry!

Noa: Don't be sorry! It's for charades! I am aMAzing at charades

Mal: 🌀 I bet! Have fun

Noa: Bye Mal

Mal: Bye Noa

Mal lowered her phone, a soft smile on her face as she saved Noa's number. She may not have a self-portrait, but at least Noa wasn't mad at her anymore. That was enough to make her happy, even if she got a zero grade on this project.

But the thought of a zero grade made Mal scrunch the fabric of her quilt into a nervous knot in her fist. She could not get a zero grade. Not with her "Perfect Daughter" label.

Mal forced her fingers open, smoothing out the quilt. She looked down at the worn fabric squares and then at the list of words. *Friendly, shy, logical, impulsive, quiet, outgoing.* An idea began to form in her mind. Mal reached for her colored pencils. Her eyes flicked from the quilt squares to the drawing paper as she shaded in colors to look like the texture of the fabric. With one of her paint pens, she wrote the word "smart" across the center of the first square. She kept going, making a square for each adjective. One had rows of tiny robots around the word "creative." Another looked like the TARDIS with the word "funny" written over the dark blue. She made one square with the Korean flag on it and wrote "Mallory" underneath and another one with the American flag and wrote her middle name, 지은 (*Ji-eun*), in careful Hangul under that. Then she cut each square into a puzzle piece and fit them inside her outline.

Mal tilted her head, examining it. She still wasn't sure that all these words really described her. But at least some parts of herself were there. Mallory added a line of blue watercolor across the top. She filled in the space underneath, using slow, drifting strokes of overlapping blue to cover all the white around the portrait. Then she stood back and looked at what she had done. The patchwork silhouette of a girl burst with color and patterns and words. She was faceless and completely underwater. Mal felt that she had probably captured herself exactly right.

Chapter Fifteen

AFTER DAD DROPPED THEM OFF ON SUNDAY night, Mom gave them all hugs that smelled clean and soft, like lilacs. Mal wanted to be glad for her and her time away. But there was a tight feeling in Mal's throat every time she looked at Mom. She'd only been in Sacramento a few days. Had that been long enough to decide to move there?

Mal pushed her way past the tangle of the double Ws and their backpacks bursting with stuffed animals and headed up to her room. When Mom came in to say good night later, Mal was trying desperately to focus on math. Her brain kept drifting to her webcomic. There was only one week left to vote. Dr.BotGirl had crept up to the top three, but the two other amateur webcomics were super popular. Maybe she could squeeze in another episode this week. One with a new robot friend for Zee who made the lights shine brighter whenever they came into a room.

"How's my favorite girl?" Mom said, leaning through the doorway.

Mal blinked, her mind jumping back to reality. She glanced from her screen full of baffling probability equations to Mom.

"Just working ahead," she said quickly. Instantly, she wanted to take it back. Why had she lied? Mom hadn't even asked her about math and here she was, blurting out the first thing that she thought Mom might want to hear no matter how far it was from being true. "I mean, I'm just—" she stammered.

"Let's see," Mom said, walking over. "Ah, working ahead in math. I should have known." She rubbed Mal's back and leaned in. "You get that math brain from me, you know," Mom said, a proud glow in her eyes.

Mal looked down, running her fingers over the seams in her quilt. "Yeah, I guess so," she mumbled.

"I applaud your motivation, Mal-Mal, but it's time for bed." Mom held out her hand. Mal closed the Chromebook and handed it to her. As Mom turned to set it on Mal's desk she paused. "What's this?"

Mal's eyes darted to her self-portrait. She'd taken it out

of the envelope when she got home, just to make sure it hadn't wrinkled. Now Mom was looking down at it, a mildly curious expression on her face. Mal felt her mouth go dry. There was her Mal-shaped outline, with everything inside it split into so many different pieces, labeled with so many different words. Would Mom look at it and understand that Mal was not just a little replica of her, with Mom's discipline and Mom's schedules and Mom's math brain?

"Just something for art," Mal said.

Mom's eyes ran over the drawing. Mal's heart seemed to pause, waiting in the still air of the room. "Hmm," Mom said. "That's very creative." She set the Chromebook down next to the portrait and turned back to Mal. "Jal ja, sweetie. It's good to have you home."

Mal squeezed her eyes shut as Mom kissed her forehead. "Good night, Mom," she said, turning on her side and pulling her quilt up. Mom switched off her light and closed the door. Mal's heart thudded painfully in her chest. Mom had looked right at the patchwork pieces of a girl who had a million different words for who she was and still no face and she hadn't *seen* it. She hadn't even recognized Mallory.

Mal's phone buzzed as she walked to school the day after break. It was a video call from Noa.

"Hi," she said, feeling that thrill she felt every time she saw Noa.

"Mal! Oh, good," Noa said. It looked like they were walking to school. Their gray-blue eyes kept darting away from their phone to look where they were going. "I need moral support. Please give me moral support."

"Always happy to," Mal said. She peered at Noa's face on the screen. They did look a bit on edge. "Um, do you need a virtual hug? A cheer? Or, like, a pep talk?"

"Yes, emergency pep talk. That would be excellent."

"Okay . . . Noa, you are a stellar performer, and you have a great voice. You are fun and kind and too good for this whole neighborhood, really." Mal looked at Noa's fitted boy's button-up shirt, suspenders, and striped bow tie. "And you look very . . . handsome?" She hoped that was the right word.

Noa grinned. Some of the tension had already left their face. "I'll definitely take handsome. *Dapper* would also be acceptable."

"Noted. Okay, so why do you need moral support right now?"

Noa's face fell again. "Mom just texted me. She said there are some people making a big deal about the story time. They've started talking about it on right wing talk shows. National ones. It's not good. She wanted me to know before I go to the library after school. I guess there might be protestors."

"Protestors? At the library?" There had been some protests in their neighborhood before. Sometimes there were marches over women's rights or Black Lives Matter. Etta went to some of those. But just last month out on Main Street there had been a small group of protestors yelling mean things about immigrants. Wendy had passed them on her bike on the way to school and was pretty shaken up the rest of the day. Still, Mal had never seen anyone protest the library.

Noa's eyes were like twin storm clouds. They nodded. "There's no Reading Buddies or comic club today, but I was still planning to go there after school. And now I'm a little nervous. I honestly just hate the thought of them"—Noa shivered—"creeping on my library."

"I'll come with you," Mal said quickly.

"Really?" Noa brightened and put a hand over their heart. "You would do that? For me?"

"Go to the library?" Mal asked. "What can I say? I take risks for my friends."

Noa laughed. "Thanks, Mal. I gotta run," Noa said. "I'll text you after school."

Mal ended the call. As she hurried up the school steps, slipping her phone into her bag, it buzzed again. She glanced at the screen.

Noa: You give great pep talks! ♥

Mal felt warm tingles pop inside her chest. Despite whatever was brewing at the library, Mal was smiling as she went inside.

_____

After lunch Mal took a detour into the bathroom by the cafeteria. She pulled her shaggy hair back in a ponytail and was splashing water on her face when K.K. came in.

"Hey, Mal," K.K. said, plopping her makeup bag on the sink and leaning forward to look in the mirror.

"Hi," Mal said, wiping down her face and reaching for her glasses. "Is it time for a reapplication?"

K.K. smiled. "You know it. Lunchtime refresh." She glanced at Mal and lifted one perfect eyebrow. "Where's yours?"

Mal shrugged. "In my locker. I'm going full natural face today." She didn't tell K.K. that she preferred natural. Instead she peered at her reflection and wrinkled her nose. "Which is kinda yikes, not gonna lie."

"I got you," K.K. said, unzipping her bag. "My mom just got some new blush samples." She handed Mal a brush and a tiny compact. "Just give yourself a smidge of color."

Mal dutifully brushed at her cheeks, trying not to cringe. She wasn't sure why, but the feeling of makeup on her skin always made her itchy. She couldn't admit that to K.K., though, not after they'd been makeup buddies for the last two months.

"Oh, hey," K.K. said as she finished up her makeup. "You know those kids Marcus and James? They said you're in a club with them?"

Mal nodded. "Um, yeah," she said casually, handing K.K.

back the blush. "It's just a thing at the library I do sometimes." Her brain fumbled, as if rearranging things. Why did it seem so weird for K.K. to know about comic club? K.K. had said before that James was helping student council make posters. And he's the one who showed K.K. *Metal-Plated Heart.*

As if reading her mind, K.K. said, "Anyway, you know that comic with the Etta robot? We keep finding other things in there about people here at school."

Mal sucked in her breath. "Oh?" She pretended to fix her messy hair, not meeting K.K.'s eyes. She'd been on Comic Koala yesterday and there were no more mysterious comments. She had hoped whoever recognized the mural had just forgotten about it.

"Yep. Remember when Yasmin was getting all annoyed with everyone about not recycling and she started leaving those passive-aggressive notes everywhere?"

Mal swallowed hard. She knew where this was going. She and Yasmin were both on the Green Team, but Yasmin took it way too far. At first Yasmin just made general recycling signs to post around school. But then she'd started leaving little sticky notes on people's lockers when she noticed them not recycling. Some people had gotten mad about it. Even Mal had been annoyed.

K.K. looked at Mal in the mirror, her eyes wide. "That scene is totally in the comic. Only it's this robot named Opie who leaves notes all over their spaceship."

Mal finally met K.K.'s eyes, trying to look skeptical. "But that can't be Yasmin. I mean, it's a robot, right?"

K.K. raised her eyebrows. "Except that the robot goes around saying, 'It's fine. Everything is totally fine,' when they are actually super annoyed at everyone." She leaned forward. "Just like Yasmin." She reached in her pocket and pulled out a folded piece of paper. "And there are all of these too."

K.K. unfolded the paper. There, scrawled out in pen was a neat list.

Smoker=Etta

Opie=Yasmin

Planet election=7th grade election

Alien candidate=Brett

Heart-eyes girl=Fiona

Zelda concert mural

DA Official=Mr. Emerson?

"That many?" Mal said. "Doesn't that seem . . . unlikely?" Her voice sounded stretched out and thin.

"There are a ton of episodes," K.K. said. "I haven't had time to read them all, but I bet there are more connections."

Mal's mouth went dry. K.K. hadn't gotten to the episode yet where Zee meets Linda, the character with perfect hair and makeup. The character that looked just like K.K. Suddenly Mal felt more aware of her overstuffed backpack than usual, as if her sketchbook were a live presence inside it clamoring to be noticed.

"We think this Dr.BotGirl goes to LPA," K.K. said.

Mal couldn't think of anything to say that would smooth all this over and brush it away. Why did they have to obsess over this? Why couldn't they just read a comic and move on? Mal took a long, slow breath, reminding herself that she didn't get mad. "I don't know. It seems like a stretch to me. I need to get to class," she said. She gave a smile that felt robotic, like she had preprogrammed it into her cybernetic jaw, and walked away, tugging on her backpack straps.

Chapter Sixteen

"DID IT HURT, THOUGH?" WINSTON'S VOICE WAS worried.

Noa fingered the feather earring. "Not really. It was just a quick poke. Kind of like a shot." Noa had caught up to Mal and the twins as they were walking to aftercare. Winston had been staring at Noa's earring the whole time, working up the courage to ask about it. Now his little face scrunched up.

"They give the bird a shot so they can take the feather?" He looked even more worried now.

"What? No. I was talking about getting my ears pierced." Noa glanced at Mal in confusion.

"I think he wanted to know if it hurt the bird," Mal whispered to them.

Noa's face cleared. "Oh!" Then it clouded again. They gave Winston a fake smile and spoke to Mal in a whisper out of the side of their mouth, trying not to move their lips. "But I don't *know* if it hurt the bird. Will your brother hate me if it did?"

"I mean, he might," Mal said, trying not to laugh. "Wyatt!" she called. "Stop climbing that fence! You know it's not allowed!" Mal turned back to Noa and realized that they looked legitimately concerned. "I'm teasing," she said quickly. "I don't think Winston is capable of hating anyone."

But just to put Noa at ease, Mal said to Winston, "Birds lose their feathers sometimes. That's just part of being healthy for them. Sometimes they need to get rid of old feathers. It's totally okay."

Winston was quiet for a moment, and Noa smiled gratefully at Mal. But then Winston asked if that meant that Noa's earring was *un*healthy since a bird lost it. By then they were at the aftercare room so Mal hurried the boys in and handed them off. When she came back out, Noa was shaking their head.

"I mean, Mom worries that my sibling isn't talking much yet, but I gotta say, I am *not* prepared for the questions. If Zephyr gets like that, I'm going to have to learn a whole lot of random stuff real quick."

"You don't have to know real answers. You just have to know what they want to hear," Mal explained. "For example, Winston wants every animal or bug everywhere to live happily ever after. So as long as you can give an answer that fits that dream"—she shrugged—"he'll love you."

"So . . . that wasn't true? What you said about birds losing their feathers?"

"I have no idea. It *sounds* true. I mean, it makes sense. And it made Winston feel better."

"Well, that seems kind of manipulative," Noa said.

Mal flinched. "I—I didn't mean it like that," she said softly. "I just want him to be happy."

"Yeah, I know that," Noa said. "I just don't think being happy is the most important thing, necessarily."

"Really?" Mal said. "Isn't that what everyone in the entire world wants, though?" She asked it lightly, but there was something about this that felt deep and important. Why wouldn't happiness be the most important thing?

"Okay," Noa said. "Imagine you could get a brain implant or something that just made you happy all the time no matter what. Would you do it?"

"Um," Mal hesitated. "Wouldn't you?"

Noa raised their eyebrows. "Happy *all* the time," they emphasized. "Like you could be starving to death and still feel happy. So you might not even eat because why bother if you're already happy?"

"Okay, I see your point," Mal admitted.

"And what about other people?" Noa continued. "If you could make everyone you loved happy all the time, so happy that they didn't even care what happened to them, would you do it?"

Mal squirmed. "No, obviously. I would not want them to die of happiness."

"Besides," Noa said, "I wouldn't want someone to lie to me just to make me happy. I'd rather they be honest with me."

Mal didn't know what to say to that. She wondered what would happen if she were totally honest with everyone in her life. Including Noa, who had just told Mal that they wouldn't want anyone to lie to them. The thought made her shiver. Mal licked her lips and said, "Yep. You are totally right."

"Why, thank you," Noa said, giving a theatrical bow.

Mal giggled, pushing her discomfort away.

Noa stopped walking. "Speaking of starving, I didn't really eat much at lunch. Want to grab some food?"

"Yeah, okay," Mal said, relieved the conversation had shifted.

"Great! What do you want?" Noa looked around. "Crack o' Dawn has sandwiches or there's the gyro place. Or pizza."

"Oh, wherever you want."

"Yeah, but what do you like?" Noa asked.

Mal looked around. Crack o' Dawn Café might not have seats inside and it was getting too cold to sit on the patio. The gyro place was a few blocks away. If Noa was really hungry, they should eat somewhere closer. Pizza Pundit was always good but there'd probably be a ton of kids from school. And she kind of wanted to hang with Noa without people she knew around. Her brain spun.

"Mal? Hello?" Noa was looking at her closely.

"Umm . . . I don't care. Really," she insisted. "Wherever you want."

Noa gave a short sigh.

"Well, okay, fine. If you don't care . . ." Their words trailed off, and Mal's fingers fiddled with the straps on her backpack. Was Noa mad at her?

"Let's do pizza!" Noa smiled. "I'm in the mood for hot and greasy."

Mal felt immediate relief. "Perfect."

"So, do you have a favorite?" Noa asked as they waited in line to give Fat Marv their order. "Mine is the Rachel. Chorizo and artichoke is an amazing combo!"

"Same!" Mal agreed.

"Miss Mallory, Captain Noa," Fat Marv called out. He gave them a sharp military salute. "What'll it be?"

"One Rachel to share, please," said Noa.

"Captain?" Mal asked as they made their way to a booth.

Noa laughed. "Yeah. Mister and miss don't really work for me, so he asked what he should call me. We tried a few different things. But I like Captain because he always salutes me when he says it."

"I like that," Mal said, lifting her hand to her forehead in a salute. "Captain."

Noa seemed way less anxious than earlier, and Mal was eager to keep them happy. They talked about favorite movies and younger siblings and school. Just as Fat Marv called their order, the door jingled and Fiona walked in with some of her friends. Mal turned her head to look out the window as Noa got up to get their pizza. She let her shaggy hair fall down to cover her face. She wasn't exactly sure why, but she didn't want Fiona to see her.

"Mal!" Fiona called. Mal took a breath and turned. Fiona was coming over.

"Hey, Fiona," Mal said.

At that moment, Noa returned and set the pizza in front of Mal. They grinned at Fiona. "Hi! I don't think I know you yet," they said. "I'm Noa. They/them."

"This is Fiona," Mal said. "She/her. I know her from school."

"Cool," Noa said. "Want to sit here? There's plenty of room."

Mal nodded, a welcoming smile on her face. But her heart was sinking.

"Sure! Sabs, get us a Jake to split," Fiona called back to her friend. She slid into the booth next to Mal. Sabs rolled her eyes at Fiona but went dutifully up to the counter.

"Want a piece of ours while you wait?" Noa asked. They waved a hand over the pizza and chorizo-scented steam drifted into the air. Fiona took one look at the pizza and twisted her lips in disgust.

"Ew, artichoke? No, thank you! I can*not* handle the texture." She put out a hand like she was warding off evil.

"Well, that is just wrong," Noa said. "I pity you, poor unfortunate soul." They lifted a slice and took a bite.

Fiona watched with a look of disbelief. "You do you, I guess," she said. Then she looked at Mal, who was reaching for a piece. Fiona's mouth tilted in confusion. "I thought you hated artichoke."

Mal widened her eyes and shook her head no. She took a big bite of the hot pizza to prove that she liked it. The piping hot sauce burned her tongue and she had to suck in air around it to cool it off. At least she didn't have to say anything with a full mouth.

Noa swallowed and said, "No, the Rachel is Mal's favorite. Artichoke and chorizo."

Fiona waved her hand dismissively. "No way. The Jake is her favorite. Same as me."

Mal concentrated on her food, ignoring the curious look Noa gave her. The taste of artichoke was worse than the burned tongue.

"So, how are you two friends?" Fiona asked.

"From the library," Noa explained. "We do comic club and Reading Buddies there."

"Oh, right." Fiona nodded. "That's why you don't come to swim anymore."

Noa looked at Mal. "I didn't know you did swim."

"Mal was on the team longer than me," Fiona said. "Until she quit this year. It's too bad because you are seriously missing out, Mallory." She giggled. "Let's just say I have a pretty fine view during warm-up stretches."

Mal wanted to be anywhere but here. She wanted to crawl out of her skin and fly away.

"What do you mean?" Noa asked.

"There are these two eighth-grade boys that are super cute," Fiona said. "Mal, I didn't tell you that I talked to Dinesh! He said his cousin might be into hanging out with us. Like a double date!" She squealed in excitement.

Any other time, Mal would have squealed back. But now all she wanted was for Fiona to leave and never mention boys to her again. Mal set down her pizza. She didn't feel so good.

Noa was staring from Fiona to Mal.

"Fiona," Sabs called, waving to her from an empty table. "There's more room over here. And Morgan is coming too."

"Ugh, Morgan," Fiona rolled her eyes. "She is such a drama queen. I'd better go. Bye, Noa. See you, Mal." She slid out of the booth and joined her friends.

Mal stared down at her pizza, afraid to meet Noa's eyes.

"So . . . ," Noa said slowly. "You swim?"

Mal nodded.

Noa finished their slice of pizza and wiped their fingers. They weren't talking much. Mal was getting some very uncomfortable vibes from them. This wasn't the fun-loving Noa that she was used to. Suddenly all Mal wanted to do was crawl in bed. Hanging out with multiple people was exhausting. On their walk to the library, Mal couldn't take the silence anymore.

"Hey, are you okay?" she asked.

Noa stopped and looked at Mal. The gray in their eyes was deeper than she'd ever seen it. It swallowed up the blue, like spilled ink. "Yeah. I just . . ." They trailed off.

"What?" Mal asked, feeling her heart speed up. "What's wrong?"

"It's weird. I feel like—I *felt* like I'd known you for a really long time. And I kind of forgot that we actually just met a couple weeks ago."

Mal swallowed. Her throat was dry. She should have drunk more water with her pizza. "I felt that too," she said. "When we first met. I felt like I knew you."

Noa nodded and kicked at the ground. "But . . ." Their voice dipped so low Mal had to lean forward. "I don't think we really know each other that well."

"But we do," Mal said quickly. "I mean, yeah, there's stuff we might not know about each other. Yet. So what?"

"Do you still want to do the lip sync?" Noa asked suddenly, looking Mal straight in the eyes.

"Of course," Mal said. "Why wouldn't I?"

"I'm not sure." Noa shrugged. "The way Fiona talked about you it was like you were a totally different person."

"Noa . . ." Mal wasn't sure what to say.

"I mean, I had this really weird moment. . . ." Noa tugged at the curls hanging over their forehead. "Sorry, it sounds stupid."

"No," Mal said, even though she wanted to stop this conversation and just go back to their comfortable pre-Fiona interactions. "Tell me."

"I looked at you and wasn't sure who you were. It was like an optical illusion or something. And what is up with those guys? Are you . . . into them or something?"

"No! That's Fiona, not me," Mal said. "I'm not into them. I'm—" She stopped herself before she could blurt out, *I'm into you.*

Noa looked at her, gray eyes steady and searching. Mal thought about falling into that gray and letting the fog carry her off.

"I'm not Fiona," Mal said firmly. "And I definitely want to do the lip sync."

Noa nodded slowly. "Okay," they said. "Well, then we really need to practice. The drag story time is this Saturday."

"Right!" Mal said, nodding. "Yes, we need to practice."

"I'd say we could practice tonight, but I have only like half an hour to finish my homework," Noa said as they headed inside. "Maybe tomorrow or Thursday? Practice after school?"

"Yeah," Mal said quickly. "That works."

They found a table in the library and both got out their Chromebooks. Mal didn't know if she was imagining the strange edge in the air. Maybe Noa was just really focused on their homework.

Noa's phone buzzed and they glanced down. "My mom's here," they said, reaching for their backpack. "Thanks for hanging out with me, Mal."

Mal felt like a deflated balloon after Noa left. She stared blankly at her math book until Barbara cleared her throat, startling her. The librarian's piercing eyes were locked on Mal. What was she doing, staring at her like that? What did Barbara care if she didn't do her math homework? Mal had a sudden urge to stick out her tongue at the older woman.

Instead, Mal forced a smile and looked down at her Chromebook again. But nothing sank in. She would never understand probability models. Besides, she didn't need a model to figure out the probability of her and Noa ever being more than friends. Noa was cool and fun and spontaneous. What would happen when they realized that Mal was not a theater kid like them? What would happen when Mal completely screwed up the lip sync? Mal took off her glasses and pressed her palms into her eyes. She didn't want Noa to think she'd been dishonest. She wanted to make their cheek dimple and watch them play with that curl that hung over their forehead.

"Math homework?" A gruff voice said. Mal lifted her head. Barbara stood next to her, looking down at her screen with a grim expression.

Mal swallowed. "Yeah. Probability models."

Barbara grunted. Then she reached in the pocket of her cardigan and took out a piece of notepaper. Leaning over the table, she wrote a website on the paper and handed it to Mal.

"There are videos on this site that walk you through every math concept. Makes it easy to understand."

Mal stared at the paper. "Thank you," she said.

Barbara nodded stiffly. "Maybe if I'd had a site like this in middle school, I wouldn't have failed math," she said, and she turned back to the desk.

Barbara the Brutal failed math? Mal thought in surprise.

The site did help, and Mal managed to struggle through a few problems before it was time to pick up the boys. She was still way behind, but at least she'd gotten something done. Thanks to Barbara, of all people. She packed her books into her bag, ready to get home and fall into bed. As she slid the piece of paper into her pencil case, Mal noticed something printed on the back.

*"If I didn't define myself, I would be crunched into other
people's fantasies for me and eaten alive."*
Audre Lorde

Eaten alive. She'd seen those words on the whiteboard the other day. Reading the whole thing now was like a flashlight shining into a dark cave. It was eerie. Like this Audre person had leaned down and peeked right into her soul.

Before she settled into bed that night, Mal found herself reaching for her sketchbook. On the last page she wrote an idea for an episode. *The DA sends their trash compactor robots after Zee to eat her alive. She has to fight back. She has to define herself.*

Chapter Seventeen

Comic Koala Direct Message
To: Dr.BotGirl
From: S.J.theBoss

Hello, Dr.BotGirl,

The Comic Koala competition ends in three days and your comic has been holding steady in the top five for your category. Congratulations! I noticed that your account information is incomplete and I'd like to rectify that before it's time to announce our winners. We are missing your guardian information and will need that to process any awards after the competition.

I also see that you are local to Columbus. I'm looking for young artists who are interested in joining an ongoing workshop that I will be launching in the next few months at my comics shop. You've created quite a fun, inclusive world in your comic, Dr.BotGirl, and I'd love to see what you do with it next. If your parent or guardian could be in touch with me, we can talk more.

Write on,

S.J. Summerhill

She/They

Mal read the message six times before she could really believe it. She even took off her glasses and blinked at the screen. But the message was still there. S.J. Summerhill congratulating her on how well her comic was doing. S.J. Summerhill inviting her to a comic workshop. The smile stretching across her face was starting to hurt when she finally stopped staring at the words. But what was she supposed to do now? She couldn't talk to her parents about it. A dark little voice whispered that she could use her mom's email to respond. If S.J. thought Mom agreed, maybe she could find a way to do the workshop.

"Mallory, let's go. You're going to be late!" her mom called up the stairs. "And don't forget your swim things!"

Mal took a deep breath and closed her Chromebook. She

tried to push away the guilt as she stuffed her swimsuit into the bag. For now she just wanted to hold on to the thought that S.J. Summerhill wanted her to take a Comic Koala workshop. She would carry this sunshiny feeling with her all day.

At first she didn't think anything of the whispers and giggles in math class. But then she heard what two girls were saying behind her.

"—just like Fiona."

"Did you see the one with Emerson?"

Mal froze, listening.

"Yes! The evil official with the bow tie and glasses?" The kid laughed and the sound was like an alarm bell in Mal's head. Her heart began to race.

Mal tried to turn casually enough to see what they were looking at but their phones were out of sight. Mal didn't get a single math problem right after that. She left class in a daze and walked numbly through the halls. Every time she saw someone sneaking a look at their phone, her heart jumped. She tried to tell herself she was being paranoid. There was no way every kid in school was reading her webcomic. Was there?

Mal ducked into the bathroom and locked herself in a stall. She usually tried not to log in to Comic Koala from her phone. It helped to keep her from checking comments too often. Now her fingers trembled as she typed in her password and tapped the notifications icon. Fourteen new comments. She skimmed them, hardly daring to breathe.

Yo, LPA represented!

This is SOOO GOOOD.

Brett's an alien!!!! I knew it!!!

Mal told herself not to panic. Dr.BotGirl had thousands of followers. What did it matter if some of them were from her school?

The bell rang, and Mal jumped. She was already handing in her self-portrait late, and now she was late to art class too. She didn't want to disappoint Miss Hill any more than she already had. But she had to know what they were saying. Mal scrolled through the rest of the comments.

Who is this Dr.BotGirl nerd?

Zee you gonna destroy all homework for us?

Guys, who is writing this!!!???

Mal felt her breathing relax. They didn't know. They may have figured out about Mr. Emerson and the "You Belong" mural and even Brett and Fiona. But no one knew who Dr.BotGirl was. Mal closed her eyes. She wanted her bed and her patchwork quilt and silence. Instead she forced herself to open the door. She imagined *Metal-Plated Heart* and the entire Comic Koala site as one big tangled ball of fluff. With each step she took, she pictured herself shoving the fluff down, pressing it into an itty-bitty container. She put one foot in front of the other, pushing and pushing the whole way to class, until the entire webcomic fiasco was wadded up in a little ball at the back of her brain. She took a deep breath and walked into art.

"Mallory, this is fantastic!" Miss Hill said, her bright eyes combing over Mal's self-portrait.

Mal looked down, a flush of pleasure creeping up her cheeks. She still felt like the patchwork girl was a thrown-together mess, but she liked the colors and the patterns. And, most important, she wouldn't get a zero grade.

"Oh, did you finish it?" Wendy asked as she and Yasmin entered the classroom. They both hurried over.

"Wow, it's so colorful," Yasmin said, leaning closer to see.

"Isn't it?" Miss Hill said. "And I love the details on each of these pieces." She ran a finger over the Korean flag with "Mallory" written underneath. Then she traced a line to the patch with the American flag and 지은 under that. "What does this say?" she asked.

"Ji-eun. It's my Korean middle name."

Miss Hill beamed. "What a lovely way to incorporate your Korean heritage. Yasmin has some Arabic on hers as well and Wendy's has Spanish. I love seeing all the different threads of culture represented in our class."

"Oh, that's the TARDIS!" Wendy exclaimed. "From *Dr. Who*."

"Look at the tiny robots," Yasmin said. "Those are so cute."

Mal stared down at the patch of paper with the row of robots along the bottom. She hadn't even realized that her robot pattern was made up of miniature versions of Smoker.

"Mallory, well done," Miss Hill said, looking up at Mal. "I'm proud of you for breaking through that creative block." She slid the portrait back into the envelope. "And just in time. I'll be displaying these in the hallway next week."

Mal had a sudden vision of James and Marcus examining her portrait with a cartoonishly large magnifying glass pointed at the robots. "Oh, could I have it back until then?" she said quickly. "Just to, uh, put a finish on it. To protect it."

"Certainly, if you like," Miss Hill said. "But I have some Mod Podge here—"

"That's okay," Mal blurted. "Sorry, I just— I have some at home." She took the envelope and followed her friends to their seats. Maybe she'd change the robots to little crowns for the drag queen story time. That wouldn't give anything away.

Wendy mouthed, *"Good job,"* as class got started, and Mal smiled back at her. But she felt uncomfortable. Her self-portrait was just a jumble of things, not some perfect representation of who she was. Maybe it was like Miss Hill had been saying in their discussions about art. Art was interactive and everyone brought their own self to it. That's why Miss Hill saw some profound cultural self-reflection, and Wendy saw her sci-fi fandom. Everyone saw what they wanted to see. But had anyone seen Mallory?

After dropping off her brothers at aftercare, Mal geared herself up for comic club. Mal decided that today she would be the fun, bubbly, lip-syncing performer extraordinaire that Noa needed. Mal was ready. But when she walked into the library someone was shouting. She froze next to the shelf of new books, staring. A man was standing in the middle of the library, his chin jutting forward and his face red. But he wasn't the one shouting. It was Barbara. The top of her head came only as high as his nose, but her presence seemed to fill the whole library.

"—out now!" she shouted. Her glasses swung on their gold-and-pearl chain and her eyes flashed. With a visible effort, Barbara took a shuddering breath and said in a lower voice, "One month. You may return in one month as long as you will follow our code of conduct."

The guy gave a disbelieving laugh and looked around. "You serious right now?"

Barbara tightened her lips and stood up straighter.

The security guard came up behind her and gestured to the door. "Let's go," he said.

Mal backed out of the way as the man stomped out, his fists clenched. "This is BS!" he yelled over his shoulder as he left.

Mal stared back at Barbara. She was watching him leave with a look of grim satisfaction. But Mal noticed that Barbara's hands were trembling as she tucked them into the pockets of her cardigan. The manager, Zachary, had been across the building when the shouting started and just now made it to Barbara. He spoke to her quietly and she answered, her face hard and tight. After a moment, Zachary gestured toward the staff door and they both walked into the back room, looking serious.

Mal looked around, her senses on high alert. Izzy and Marcus were watching from the teen area. Mal saw Lucy nearby and went up to her.

"What happened?" Mal asked.

"I'm not sure," Lucy said, looking worried. "He was over by the desk. And then they started arguing."

Mal shivered. "I can't imagine getting on her bad side."

Lucy made a humph sound. "Sure, but imagine what being on her good side is like." It was a valid point. Still, the Barbara blowup had left a bad feeling on Mal's skin, like just watching it had infected her somehow.

"I wonder what that guy did?" Izzy said, coming over. "Bring a book back late?"

"Barbara doesn't kick people out over late books," Lucy said sharply. "She's probably forgiven more fines than anyone else who works here."

"Really?" Mal asked. "She seems so tough."

"Oh, she *is*. Life's thrown some hard stuff at her, but she's a survivor. I am going to go check on her, though. Regardless of what you might think, her skin isn't as thick as it seems." Before she left, Lucy looked at Mal and Izzy. "Don't judge a book by its cover, you two. You should know that by now."

They watched her leave. Izzy made a face before going back to talk to Marcus. A little stubborn part of Mal didn't want to think about Barbara being a survivor or being upset. But she still had an itch of curiosity about what had made the librarian so mad.

"Hey."

Noa was standing behind her. Even with the tension still hanging in the air, Mal felt her heart lift at the sight of Noa.

"Hey!" she said. "Did you see Barbara rip into that guy? What do you think happened?"

Noa looked at the floor. Mal slowly noticed that their face was pale and they seemed unsettled.

"What's up?" she asked Noa.

Noa shot their eyes toward the door. They lifted one shoulder uncomfortably.

"That guy . . ." Noa blew their breath out in a quick huff. "He . . . said something to me."

"What?" Mal took a step closer. "That guy that Barbara kicked out? What did he say?"

"He said . . ." Noa hesitated, not meeting Mal's eyes. "He said, 'Oh, you aren't a he. What are you, then, an *it*?' And then he just . . ." They swallowed. "Laughed. He thought it was funny."

Their eyes shone with tears and Mal's heart ached.

"He called you '*it*'?" Mal asked.

Noa nodded. "I mean, it's not the first time anyone's said that." Mal felt sick at the thought. How could anyone be that horrible? Noa swallowed. "But he wouldn't stop saying 'it' even when I asked him."

"You asked him?" Mal was incredulous. She would never have asked a dude like that to stop. She would have just waited him out.

"Well, it didn't matter anyway," Noa said. "Because then Barbara came out of nowhere."

Suddenly their eyes shone with admiration.

"She told him people's humanity isn't up for debate. She actually said"—Noa laughed—"she actually said that books build empathy, and he obviously must not be much of a reader."

"No way!" Mal laughed. "Whoa, roasted by Barbara the Brutal. That should teach him."

Noa's smile fled their face. "Don't call her that."

Mal looked at them and nodded. "Oh yeah, I just meant . . . I mean, she defended you!"

"That's right," Noa said seriously. "She defended me, and she is awesome."

"Okay," Mal said. "She is awesome."

"People need to be nicer to her!" Noa said. "Did you know her cat went missing last week? And the cat was pretty much all she had. She doesn't have any family. Can you imagine? I think I would lose my mind without other people."

Mal nodded in agreement, although the idea of being able to go home to no one else who wanted to watch something different or eat something else sounded magical.

"You are completely and totally right," Mal said. "I guess I just . . . I don't know. She seems like the grumpy villain type."

Noa was still frowning. "Well, she's not," they snapped. They sniffed and rubbed at their eyes.

"Okay, she's not," Mal agreed. She decided immediately that Barbara would never again end up as a villain in her comic. In fact, if Noa wanted her to, she'd make a hero version of Barbara who joined forces with Zee in her revolution against injustice. "I'm really glad she stood up to that guy," Mal said. Then she added thoughtfully, "Barbara the Brilliant."

Noa looked up at her and gave a watery smile.

"Or Barbara the Bold?" they suggested.

"Perfect," Mal said. She was so glad to see that dimple again. In a quieter voice she asked, "Are you okay?"

Noa nodded and lifted their head. "For sure. Ignorance is everywhere. I can't let it get me down."

"Yeah," Mal said, making her voice upbeat, "Barbara the Brave wouldn't want you to give in to despair."

Noa laughed.

At that moment the staff door opened and Barbara herself, stern glare firmly in place, stepped back out. Mal and Noa froze. The librarian's eyes landed on them. She gave Noa a piercing look that made Mal want to shrink away. But Noa beamed at her and said, so quietly that Barbara probably had to read their lips, "Thank you."

Barbara's face softened. She nodded to Noa, a simple recognition, and headed to the desk. Mal let out her breath slowly, feeling as if a story line had been rewritten.

"Hey, we have *got* to practice," Noa said suddenly, grabbing her hand. They pulled Mal with them toward Lucy's office. "We're in a total time crunch!"

Maybe Noa was just trying to overcompensate for their emotions earlier, but they practically pulsed with excitement. They insisted on singing each line out loud to get the timing right. Noa's voice was clear and high, and made Mal's heart rise up like a feather on a gust of wind. Mal, on the other hand, was pretty sure that if she sang along, the potted plant in Lucy's office might shrivel up and die. Noa's energy was infectious. Soon Mal was twirling around in a silver-and-blue tutu with the white faux fur wrapped around her shoulders. She did her best to follow Noa's choreography, but the office was too small and Noa kept adding more props. Also, they both kept dissolving into laughter.

"Stop it!" Noa said, crossing their arms and giving Mal a playful glare.

Mal nodded and clasped her hands behind her back, biting her lip to keep from laughing. It was difficult because Noa was wearing the tangerine tutu and a platinum-blond wig cut in a bob. They were also holding a sandwich.

"Okay, time to take this seriously!" Noa said. Every time they started smiling, they pulled their lips back in a kind of almost frown that made their cheek dimple. "What?" Noa asked.

Mal realized she had been staring at their dimple, and she panicked. "Yeah. Good. Serious. Yes!" Mal gave Noa a thumbs-up. *Wow, what was that?* she thought. *A caveman impression?* Noa didn't seem to notice.

"Get in position!" they called.

Mal rearranged her fur and sat on the book cart, ready to go. When Noa gave the signal, Mal tapped her phone and the music to "Love Is an Open Door" rang out in the office.

Mal had pored over the lyrics last night and again this morning. She had the words down almost perfectly. But getting the motions right was harder, especially when they got to the line about sandwiches and Noa pretended to devour the sandwich like Cookie Monster. Mal had to sit down, she was laughing so hard.

Noa looked down at the bits of bread scattered on the floor around Mal. "Whoops." They sat next to her and said in a dramatic voice, "Sometimes, I simply *become* the part."

"Or you were just hungry." Mal giggled.

"Well, we got the first part down at least," Noa said. "And the jinx part is next. Remember, we start with our right hands." Noa put out the pinkie finger of their right hand and waited. "Come on," they motioned for Mal to do it too. "Let's walk through it."

Mal, still holding back her laughter, shifted around on the floor to face Noa. She held out her right pinkie finger and Noa hooked theirs around it. Mal's skin tingled. She wondered if Noa felt it too.

"So, we say, 'jinx,' and do this," Noa said, their eyes focusing intently on their linked pinkies. "Then 'jinx again' and do the left hand." They held up their left pinkie finger.

Mal licked her lips. They'd done this part quickly before, with the music playing. But now the song had ended, and they were sitting on the floor, facing each other. She reached across and linked her left pinkie around Noa's. They held their hands suspended between them. Neither of them moved. Mal's heart raced. She was afraid to look at Noa. But her eyes moved up anyway, like a magnet was pulling them. Noa's deep gray-blue eyes were wide open, and they were looking at her as if they were drawn to her eyes too. They were looking at her as if she were something special. There was a moment that was forever and also over in an instant. It was forever because Mal couldn't believe it was really happening. She couldn't believe she was leaning toward Noa and Noa was leaning toward her. Then she felt Noa's lips press against hers. They were soft and electric. Then the instant passed, and they pulled away from each other, embarrassed. Mal felt dazed. The office door was open. There were library workers right outside. What were they thinking?

Noa must have had a similar thought because they jumped to their feet and looked out the door. When they turned around, their face was flushed, and they didn't meet Mal's eye.

"So, um, I think maybe that's enough practice for tonight," they said.

Mal nodded. She wasn't sure she could trust herself to speak. They put their costumes away without saying anything. *Was it terrible?* Mal wondered, suddenly worried. She'd never kissed anyone before. Not really. Except once on a dare, but that didn't count. Had she done something wrong? Maybe Noa hated it. She shot a sidelong glance at Noa. Noa was doing the same thing. Their eyes locked, and they both looked away quickly.

"Jinx," Noa said in a very quiet voice.

Mal snorted, and suddenly they were both laughing. She was relieved to see their dimple again.

Her phone rang. Reluctantly, she looked away from Noa and glanced at the screen.

It was her dad. *Oh no.* Today was Wednesday. It felt like a lifetime ago that she had told Dad they could do pizza this week on Wednesday.

"Sorry, Noa, gotta run!" Mal leaped to her feet and lunged for the door.

"Um, okay, bye," Noa called after her.

Mal rushed through the staff room and toward the front, answering the call as she went.

"Hello?"

"Hi, Pumpkin!" her dad's cheerful voice called. "I just parked. Are you done with practice?"

"Oh yeah," Mal panted as she stepped out of the library. She shot a glance across to the parking lot. Did she have time to get through the community center doors before her dad saw her? "Just out of breath from swimming."

"Coach is pushing you, huh?"

"Yeah, lots of laps." Mal spotted his car and backed up. She'd have to wait until he went in and then run across. Her heart was racing. "I still gotta change. Can you get the boys first?"

"Sure thing. See you soon!"

Mal pocketed her phone and then nearly jumped as she heard Noa's voice from behind.

"Who was that?"

Noa was holding Mal's backpack, and they were staring at her.

"Uh, my dad," she said, her mouth dry.

Noa frowned. "Your dad thinks you're swimming?"

Mal didn't know what to say. She looked from Noa's face

to the parking lot where her dad was getting out of his car. Noa's frown deepened.

"You forgot your backpack," they said, holding it out.

Mal took it. Noa was staring at Mal like they weren't sure what to think, and she suddenly remembered Noa saying they would rather people be honest with them. She looked down at her backpack. It felt even heavier than usual.

"Thanks," she mumbled.

"Sure," Noa said. They gestured to her backpack. "Did you know there's a hole?"

"Yeah," Mal said. Her fingers went to the front pocket. "It's been there awhile."

"There's a bigger one," Noa said. "On the side."

Mal frowned and felt along her backpack. Noa was right. The seam had torn, and she could feel her swim towel through the opening. "Oh, thanks," she said, shifting it to make sure nothing fell out. She glanced outside again and saw her dad pass by, heading to the center doors. She could feel Noa's eyes on her.

"Okay," Noa said uncertainly. "So, we'll practice again tomorrow?"

"Yes, definitely!" Mal said. She desperately wanted Noa to stop looking at her like they didn't know who she was. And she desperately needed to get into the community center while her dad was in the aftercare room. Everything felt desperate and miserable. "I'll be there tomorrow. I promise."

Noa gave a small smile. Their cheek didn't dimple. "Okay, Mal. See you." They walked inside.

Mal took a deep breath and ran across the courtyard, her backpack clutched in her arms.

Chapter Eighteen

MAL HAD THE PRESENCE OF MIND TO STICK HER head under the bathroom sink in the rec center so her hair would be wet when she met Dad. She was proud of herself for thinking of that. But then she pictured Noa's frown, and her gut twisted. At least her dad seemed too busy keeping the boys under control during dinner to ask Mal many questions.

In her room later Mal unloaded her backpack to examine the damage. It was a bigger hole than she'd realized, and her towel shoved up against the tear was the only reason everything hadn't fallen out. Tears stung her eyes, and Mal blinked furiously. She didn't want to cry over a torn backpack, even if it was her favorite. She shouldn't have forgotten it when she ran out of the library. Then Noa never would have overheard her lying to her dad and the only thing on her mind right now would be that kiss. And instead of this twisting in her stomach she'd still have that floaty, bubbly feeling. Mal wiped at her eyes and got to work. Five safety pins later and she didn't feel any better. But at least her backpack looked like it might be okay for a little longer.

Mal sighed and began repacking her bag. She put in her binder first and lifted the backpack to make sure the hole didn't pull open again. The safety pins held. Mal added her books, her water bottle, and her TARDIS pencil case. She reached for her sketchbook and froze. It wasn't there.

Mal looked over the pile of things on her floor, rummaging through granola bars and extra socks. She flung her swimsuit and towel aside and checked inside her bag three times. Her sketchbook wasn't anywhere. The tear ran partway up the side, right next to the seam where it was hard to see. And it was big enough for her sketchbook to slip through. It must have fallen out before her swim towel shifted up against the hole. How had she not noticed? When had it happened? And where, she thought, feeling something dark loom up inside her, was her sketchbook now?

The next day Mal checked all her classrooms and the Lost and Found, but there was no sign of her sketchbook. She wore her ripped backpack in front of her, arms wrapped around it to make sure the repair job held up. It felt strangely comforting, like a hug.

Etta's voice broke through her thoughts.

"Mal! I heard all about the story time thing!" Etta rushed up to her, her face scrunched in worry. "I am *so* sorry! Are they still doing it?"

Mal frowned at Etta. "What do you mean? The drag queen story time? Why wouldn't they?"

"Didn't you see the news last night?" Etta asked.

Etta was the only seventh grader Mal knew who watched the news.

"No, I didn't," she told her.

Etta's words poured out fast, the way they always did when she was worked up about something. "You know that talk show? With that dude who's always yelling about things? He said the story time wasn't going to happen. He kept talking about how their group was organizing all kinds of protests and letter-writing campaigns and how they 'wouldn't stand for this corruption of the youth' or whatever."

"Wait, what? I was at the library last night. There weren't any protestors or anything."

"That's because they are not even from here." Etta gritted her teeth. "There's probably, like, one person from our town who got mad and wrote into that ridiculous show. And it's national. So of course now there are people from all these other places who think their job is to stop this. He yelled about liberal poison in our libraries and how kids are getting confused and don't know the difference been a man and a woman anymore and—" Etta's words cut off abruptly as she snapped her mouth shut.

"What?" Mal asked.

"I won't repeat it, but he said some awful stuff about drag queens," she said darkly. "And Lola is so excited. She keeps picking a different outfit to wear. If they cancel it and disappoint my baby sister . . ." Etta narrowed her eyes and made a sound almost like a growl.

"I—I'm sure they won't cancel it?" Mal said.

"But the reporter said the group had support from the Ohio House of Representatives! If the government tells the library not to do it, then they'll probably have to listen." Etta said, her face grim.

Mal could barely get any food down at lunch. Her stomach was tied into what felt like the queen of all knots, a knot made out of other knots, all of them made of steel cables. Etta ranted about freedom of speech all through lunch, and Wendy had to keep reminding her to eat. Wendy also told Mal, in her usual logical way, that there would always be haters but to focus on the supporters instead. *Great sentiment*, Mal thought. *But that won't magically make me able to get up in front of a crowd.* The more she thought about the protestors, the more certain she was that she could not go through with their performance. But the last thing she wanted was to tell that to Noa.

She worried about Noa all day. Would Noa have heard the things the talk show host had said about drag? Would they have heard what he said about kids not knowing the difference between men and women? Mal felt sick. Noa was Noa. They wouldn't be who they were if they tried to make themselves more a girl or more a boy. But there would always be people who didn't see it that way.

Mal trudged to social studies, hugging her bag. A sharp pain stabbed her finger, and she jerked her hand away from her backpack. One of the safety pins had popped open. She groaned and changed direction, heading to her locker instead. Carrying her backpack around all day was starting to feel ridiculous. But when she opened her locker, it was full of cardboard tubes and foil and other materials for Wendy's science project. Mal took a deep breath. *It's fine*, she told herself. She liked having her things with her anyway. She closed the locker and turned around, ready to hurry to class.

"Oh, good, there you are," K.K. said, making a beeline toward her. "I'm starving. Do you have anything?"

Mal blinked at her friend. "We just had lunch," she said, unzipping her backpack.

"Yeah, but Ari wanted me to show her how to do her eyeliner and it took way longer than I thought it would." K.K. glanced at the clock impatiently. Mal pulled out a granola bar and handed it to K.K., flashing her a weak smile.

"Thanks," K.K. called over her shoulder. She already had it unwrapped before Mal had time to zip her bag shut.

For some reason Mal didn't have the warm feeling she usually got from helping her friends. Instead she felt prickly inside. Like the safety pins on her backpack that kept popping open. Had K.K. really spent the entire lunch period doing makeup in the bathroom? And did she do that only because she knew Mal would have something for her to eat? How long was Wendy going to use Mal's locker? Would Yasmin ever give her back her calculator? She adjusted her grip on the backpack and gritted her teeth.

All through her next class, the prickly feeling grew, mixing with worry about the drag story time. Her brain was stuck on a loop of awful things. The guy on the TV. The mom who thought her son shouldn't read *Pinkalicious*. The man Barbara had kicked out of the library. She pictured that man standing at the back of the room while Shuga Toast read books to kids. She imagined him multiplying like cartoon clones until a crowd of people filled the room and yelled, "Corrupting the youth!" And then she thought of herself, dancing and lip-syncing with Noa in front of them all.

Mal's hand shot in the air. She asked to be excused, and hurried from the classroom. Her stomach was churning, and she was certain she was going to vomit. The nurse took one look at her and sat her down with a throw-up bag. Mal was so pale and shaky that the nurse let her stay in her office for the whole period. Mal didn't complain. She couldn't imagine getting through the rest of the day. The thought of the drag queen story time hung over her. It had been so much fun practicing with Noa. But the real thing wasn't just the two of them in Lucy's office. The real thing was them in their ridiculous outfits, lip-syncing in front of people. But it was supposed to be for a bunch of little kids. Not crowds of protestors.

When the nurse finally got ahold of her, Mal's mom went down her checklist of questions in typical Mom fashion. Did Mal have a fever? No. Was she throwing up? No. Was it something infectious? Probably not. Each question made Mal feel a bit smaller. She felt a ray of hope when Mom asked to talk to her.

"My poor darling," her mom said. "Are you all right?"

"Yeah, I just feel a little shaky."

"Mmmm . . . I wonder if your father . . . Oh, that's right, he's out of town today." Her mom's voice sounded distant now, as if she were looking away from the phone. Mal could picture her, sitting up perfectly straight, her legs crossed elegantly.

"All right," her mom said. "Okay. Let me think." Mal thought she heard her tapping her pen against the desk. She was probably swinging one foot back and forth. "I have that meeting at two thirty. Maybe if I come now . . . Oh, but I need to be in the one o'clock. . . ." She wasn't talking to

Mal. But Mal, hearing her mom try to rearrange her whole day and all her important meetings, felt a cord inside her stretching tight like a rubber band.

"Mom, it's okay," she said quickly.

"No, no, I'm coming," her mom said. She sounded distracted. "I just need to figure out when."

"Really, I'm fine. I think I'm just tired. I didn't sleep well." Mal had slept like a rock, as usual. "I can make it, Mom. Do . . ." She hesitated, not wanting to ask. Her mom had so much on her plate. "Do you think you could come home a little early, though?"

"Oh, Mallory," her mom said. "Are you sure? If you think you can make it to the end of the day, I can come home as soon as that two-thirty meeting is over. I can cancel aftercare and you can walk the boys straight home and go right to bed. I can meet you there."

Mal tried to smile. It didn't work, but she hoped it would sound like she was smiling on the phone at least. "Of course, Mom. Thanks."

Mal should have just stayed in the nurse's office. The nurse told her she didn't have to go to gym class, but then Mal realized that the locker room was the one place she hadn't looked for her sketchbook. She got there before most of the girls, but Fiona and Yasmin were already there, whispering in the corner.

"It has to be!"

"Should we tell her?"

The two girls were bent over something, but they looked up as soon as Mal walked in.

"Mal," Fiona said, motioning her over. "Come check this out!" She bit her bottom lip excitedly.

"What?" Mal asked, walking closer. She sucked in a breath. There it was, wide open on the locker room bench. Her sketchbook. Fiona had opened it up to one of the pages in the very back. They were looking at her notes.

"It's that webcomic people are talking about," Yasmin said, her eyes wide. "You know how K.K. has been all upset about that one character?"

Mal froze. She could feel her mental gears trying to turn, trying to connect things.

"What?" she said, her voice sounding very far away.

"The one with her face," Fiona said. "Didn't she show you?"

Mal shook her head slowly.

"Here," Yasmin said, pulling out her phone. She tapped at the screen and passed it to Mal. It was a scene from "Episode 14: Frills and Skills," where Linda lectures Zee about needing a makeover to infiltrate a fancy party. "*But looks* are *everything*," Linda was saying, her robotic hand waving a makeup brush.

"Um, what is that?" Mal asked weakly.

"Look at her face," Fiona said.

"See?" Yasmin's fingers moved over the screen, zooming in on Linda's face. "It's this pretty Black girl with those wavy edges just like K.K. does her hair."

"And K.K. is upset?" Mal asked slowly.

"Oh yeah." Yasmin nodded. "This girl in the comic is like image-obsessed and always trying to give makeovers. K.K. is not happy about it."

"And then," Fiona said, her voice rising in excitement. "I found this!" She jabbed her finger at Mal's sketchbook. "It totally belongs to whoever is writing this comic!"

"Oh," Mal said. Her throat felt thick.

"These notes prove it." Yasmin tapped her finger on the page and read aloud, "'K—uses makeup as power. Linda has to look perfect and she tries to push it on everyone else too.'"

"That is so harsh," Fiona squealed. "K.K. is going to be super mad."

No, no, no! Mal's brain screamed. K.K. was good at makeup and hair. Her tutorials were popular because she understood how to use that stuff. It *was* a kind of power, but Mal had always respected that about her. The notes alone made her sound shallow and vain and manipulative.

"Has she seen it?" Mal asked, her heart racing.

"She's at a student council meeting," Fiona said. "But we are definitely showing this to her as soon as she comes down here."

"And she's not the only one," Yasmin said. "Look!"

She was pointing to a note Mal had written weeks ago. *E—loses her mind when she's mad. If she had fuses, she'd blow them every other day. Smoker's fuses need constant repair.*

They were both watching her, waiting for her response, but Mal couldn't speak.

"Remember? 'Full speed ahead'?" Yasmin pointed to the E on the note. "It actually *is* Etta. Someone based it on her!" She tapped her finger triumphantly on the page.

"Definitely," Fiona said with a nod.

"The question is," Yasmin said, "who else are these notes about?"

Oh no. Mal swallowed hard. "I don't know if that's—" she tried to say, but Fiona was already leaning forward eagerly.

"Oh my god, you're right! These are probably all LPA people!"

Fiona read aloud, "'W—has to know the percentage risk of everything before acting. Tack gets stuck in processing mode.'"

"W . . . Could that be Will? From art?" Yasmin said, looking at Mal.

"Or Willow? Or— Oh!" Fiona suddenly sat straight up and waved her hands in front of her. "I know! It's—"

"Wendy," a quiet voice interrupted.

They all whirled around to see Wendy standing behind them. She had a perfect view of the sketchbook. But her dark eyes were locked on Mallory.

Mal's throat was dry. She didn't think she could speak.

Yasmin looked from Wendy to the sketchbook. "Wait," Yasmin said slowly. "So Wendy is Tack, the ship's brain?"

"I don't know," Wendy said, her voice sharp. "Does Tack get stuck being logical and never actually do anything? Does Tack slow everyone down because she wants to plan everything out first?" Wendy crossed her arms and glared at Mal.

Yasmin's eyes widened. She looked from Wendy to Mal and realization dawned on her face.

Mal shook her head and tried to speak. "No." It came out like a croak.

"No?" Wendy asked, her lips tightening. "Why? Because"—she lifted her fingers and made air quotes around the words— "'being logical is a good thing'?"

Mal's stomach twisted. *Yes*, she wanted to say. *That is all true! That's why Tack is so important!* But Wendy's face was so hurt and angry and Mal didn't think she could explain. Yasmin looked down at the sketchbook again, then back at Mal.

"You?" Yasmin asked. "You wrote the Etta robot and the heart-eyes girl?"

"Mallory?" Fiona gasped. Then she added, "What heart-eyes girl?"

"And what Etta robot?"

Mal turned panicked eyes toward Etta, who had come over to stand next to Wendy. Yasmin was flipping through the pages now, as if looking for something. Then she stopped, and Mal held her breath.

"'Y,'" Yasmin read quietly, her lips pursing together, "'says things are fine even when she's mad.'" Yasmin looked up at Mal and there was no mistaking the look on her face. Even Yasmin wasn't going to let this slide.

"What's going on?" Etta said, crossing her arms. She looked confused more than anything else, but Mal knew what was coming. They were going to tell Etta everything and show her the notes. Everyone would know all about *Metal-Plated Heart* and Smoker and Tack and Zee. Fiona would know about the heart-eyes girl who falls for the charming evil alien just like she fell for Brett. K.K., who was already angry, would be here any minute. And they would show her the notes and she would know exactly who had drawn Linda. Mal whimpered. She looked down at the sketchbook sitting open in front of Yasmin. Then Mal lurched forward, snatched up the sketchbook, and ran.

"Wait," she heard someone call, but she didn't stop. A girl by the door reached out, grabbing for her, and got a handful of her backpack. Mal tugged herself away and felt another safety pin pop open. She ran, clutching her sketchbook against the backpack as if she could hold the seams of herself together. She felt like a lumbering, alien creature as she stumbled back into the nurse's office, collapsed on the cot, and buried her face in her hands.

Chapter Nineteen

BY THE TIME MAL PICKED UP HER BROTHERS, everything in her was stretched tight. Someone in their kindergarten class had told the twins about parkour. Wyatt spent the whole walk home trying to jump off walls, bike stands, and anything else they passed, Winston following close behind. When Wyatt tried to climb on top of a recycling bin in the alley they were passing, Winston was the one who yelled at him to stop. Mal turned to see what was happening, but it was too late. The bin crashed over, spilling empty milk jugs and beer cans onto the pavement. Mal groaned.

"You're gonna make Mal mad," Winston said in a small voice.

"No, I'm not!" Wyatt said loudly. "Mal never gets mad! Besides it was an accident!"

Mal stooped to pick up a milk jug and the weight of her backpack nearly tipped her over. The irritation bubbling inside her grew and she hiked the straps up with a hard jerk. It was the last straw. The safety pins ripped free completely and her precious, worn-out backpack split wide open. Everything tumbled out. Her towel, swimsuit, homework, and granola bars scattered onto the street. Her water bottle hit the pavement with a clang.

Winston made a small "Oooooooh" sound and Wyatt yelled, "Whoops!"

Mal's hands trembled. She felt shockingly light, as if something inside her had emptied. She let out a huff of air and closed her eyes. For a moment she just stood there, not moving, reaching for the deep cave inside herself. With a Herculean effort, Mal wrestled her emotions back in check. She could do this. She could keep that band in her heart from snapping. This was her superpower.

"Okay," she said slowly, and opened her eyes. She looked at the boys. "Let's get this cleaned up."

When they got home, their mom's car was already in the driveway. Mal shifted her books and water bottle to one arm as she opened the door. She could hear her mom on the phone as they came in, the boys helpfully carrying the rest of her things. She set her stuff down and was about to go upstairs and fall into bed after this terrible, horrible, no-good, very bad day when she heard what her mom was saying.

"No, I know nothing about that!" Mom said, turning to Mal. Her eyes were like daggers pinning Mal in place. "You're telling me she hasn't been to practice in *weeks*?" Mom said in a barely controlled voice.

Oh no.

Mal could hear Coach Perkins yelling through her mom's phone. The sound tugged at the edges of that band inside her, stretching it even thinner. Her mom turned her back on her, speaking in a clipped, professional tone. She appreciated the information, and she would deal with it right away. Mal couldn't bear it. The tension was spreading through her chest. Mal took a step toward the stairs.

"Oh no you don't, young lady!" Mom was off the phone now, and her face was a storm. "I called to let your coach know you wouldn't be at practice today and I find out that you only went *twice*?" Mom's voice rose, and Mal felt that stubborn darkness inside her rise with it. "You never said anything to me about library commitments. So where have you been those days? Hanging out at the park? Wandering around the neighborhood? I only hope you have been picking your brothers up on time from aftercare!"

Mal took a shuddering breath. She needed to get away. She needed the cave. She needed her covers. Or the band inside her was going to snap. If it did, she didn't think she'd be able to put it back together. If it snapped, the backlash would sting everyone around her.

Something light and pointy hit the side of Mal's face. She blinked and looked down. It was a paper airplane.

"Sorry!" Wyatt yelled, racing across the room to retrieve his airplane. Mal bent to pick it up.

"Would you boys *please* settle down?" Mom said, her voice rising again. The volume level in this house was hitting Mal like waves, like thunder, like the walls of a trash compactor closing in on her. She lifted the paper airplane and held it out to Wyatt, but her hand froze in the air. She stared at the edge of the paper. A perforated edge, torn from a sketchbook. *No,* she thought. Very slowly, almost as if she were sleepwalking, Mal unfolded the paper airplane and stared at the smudged drawing of her latest comic. Her hand started to shake.

Mal's eyes narrowed behind her glasses, and she looked up at Wyatt. He stood in front of her, waiting with his hand stretched out.

"Wyatt," she said in a deadly quiet voice. "You took this from my sketchbook."

The smile on Wyatt's face fell away, and his eyes went from Mal to Mom and back.

"And," Mal continued. The band inside snapped. "You

turned it INTO A PAPER AIRPLANE! I do EVERY-THING for you, every single day! EVERYTHING! I pick you up from school and I make you dinner and I listen to your STUPID stories and I play your STUPID games and I keep you happy NO MATTER WHAT and it's still not enough so now you TAKE MY STUFF?!"

Wyatt's eyes were so huge they looked like a manga drawing. Behind him Winston dropped down behind the armchair, his face terrified.

"Mallory," Mom said sharply, "that's enough!"

Mal whirled toward her. "Really?" she screamed. "You want me to just step back and let them ruin my life? Just like I let you?" Her tears overflowed, and she rubbed them away angrily. She saw her mom pull back, stunned, but she kept going. "You want to know where I am for that sliver of time when I'm not doing *your* job?" Her mom's expression flooded with hurt, but Mal couldn't stop. "You have no idea what I do after school and you know why? Because you NEVER asked me what I wanted to do! You just signed me up!"

"Mallory, what are you—?" Mom started to say, but Mal cut her off.

"I HATE SWIM TEAM! And I'm not your nanny!" Mal wanted to stop so much, but the words were coming out on their own. Like shadow monsters pouring from a nightmare cave. "I was sick today, Mom." Mal wiped angrily at her face. "*I* was sick. Your *daughter*, not your babysitter. I wasn't *calling off work*! I was calling because I needed you! And instead I end up with these TERRORS—"

"Stop, Mallory! Geumanhae!" Her mom's voice lashed out, slamming a door shut on Mal's next words. Mal looked at her mom's face and then her brothers' wide eyes. A needle of guilt stabbed through her rage.

"That is *enough*! Go to your room!" Mom's voice shook. Winston started to wail. "You stay in your room until I come and deal with you!" she called to Mal over the sound. Mom hurried over to Winston and Wyatt, gathering them in her arms. As Mal watched her comfort them, she had a sudden, sharp realization—Mom was protecting her brothers *from her.*

She felt the air rush out of her and suddenly her limbs were limp and heavy. She didn't have the energy to yell anymore. She barely had the energy to stand. "I needed you," she whispered. And then she turned and stumbled to her room, tears pouring down her face.

Chapter Twenty

HER MOM CAME IN THAT NIGHT JUST LONG enough to tell her she was grounded. She tried to talk to Mal, but Mal was so deep in the dark cave inside herself that she couldn't find any words other than "I'm sorry." It wasn't enough. She knew it wasn't. She had hurt Mom and scared the boys and she couldn't just say, "I'm sorry," and fix things.

She couldn't find words for Noa either. Mal knew she couldn't meet them but explaining why felt impossible. She didn't think she could even pick up her phone. So she slept instead. She slept through the evening and the night. The next morning, she still couldn't get up. As soon as her brain dragged itself out of sleep, the memories of last night came. Memories of screaming at her mom and her brothers. Of the paper plane made from her sketchbook. Of her mom talking to Coach Perkins and her ruined backpack. Of everyone at school finding out about her comic and the protestors at the library. And Noa.

Blearily, she reached for her phone. There were twelve new texts from Noa and two missed calls.

Noa: Hey, Magnificent! You running late?

I got a great new idea. It might be snow-related.

You'll love it.

Can't wait to show you.

It's super late you coming???

Where are you!!??

I feel like something's wrong, text me!

I don't know what's going on.

It's already too late anyway, guess we won't get to practice. So that's fine.

You could have at least let me know

This was important to me

I kind of hope your sick or desperately injured bc if there's not some travesty keeping you away, then that actually sucks.

Text me, k? Good night

Mal had totally stood Noa up. And right after that kiss. All because she was too scared to go through with a performance and too chicken to admit it. Noa already thought she was a liar after overhearing her phone call with her dad. Now Noa knew Mal was a coward too. So much a coward that she hadn't even told Noa that she couldn't perform at the drag queen story time.

Mal pulled the covers back over her head. She knew she had to get up and get ready for school, but her mind didn't seem to be connected to her body. Everything was fuzzy, like being underwater, and all Mal wanted to do was sleep.

Mom finally gave up and let her stay in bed. Mal heard her moving around in the hall long after she should have left for the office. She must have taken the boys to school and then come home. The next time Mal woke up, there was a warm bowl of dakjuk on her bedside table. Mom had topped it with shredded chicken too, just how she liked it. Guilt throbbed inside her at the thought. After the way she had yelled at Mom last night, she didn't deserve dakjuk. Mal ate methodically and then dragged herself out of bed to lock the door. She didn't want to talk to her mom. Instead she reached for her laptop. *Doctor Who* was what she needed right now. She knew this wouldn't last. She would have to get up eventually. But for now, Mal stayed under her covers, glad she wasn't outside on the cold, rainy last day of November.

The knock came later that afternoon. Mal had fallen asleep again and she jolted up in bed. She stared around her room wildly, trying to grab on to something that made sense.

"Mallory?" It was her dad. He knocked on her door again, and the sound brought Mal back to reality. She was in her own room. She had skipped school. She had blown up at her family. And her dad was upstairs in their house for the first time since the divorce. "Mallory?" he called again. "Please unlock your door."

Mal got out of bed. She watched her hand lift the latch and slide it open as if it belonged to someone else. Then she turned and dragged herself back into bed. She heard her dad come in, but her head was already under the covers.

The bed sank as her dad sat next to her.

"What are you doing here?" she asked, her voice muffled.

"Your mom called me. She didn't want you home alone."

Mal pulled the covers down. Her eyes were still red and puffy. "That's why you're here? Because I'm such a bad daughter that she doesn't trust me home alone?"

"No. Because she loves you and she is worried about you. And so am I."

Mal sniffed. She had an impulse to tell her dad not to worry. But that would be ridiculous. She was not okay at all.

Dad sighed. "I heard about swim. It's that new coach,

238

right? Too much yelling?"

Mal looked away. It sounded like such a silly thing when he said it out loud.

"Did I ever tell you about my first job?" Dad asked.

"At the bookstore?" Mal had heard him tell stories about that.

"Nope. Before that. I bagged groceries for one day."

Mal raised her eyebrows. "One day?"

Her dad smiled. "Yep. My supervisor yelled at me for bagging them wrong. So I just never went back." He shrugged. "Classic conflict avoidance."

"Why is it so wrong to want to avoid conflict?" Mal mumbled, picking at the blanket.

"It's not always," Dad said. "But if avoiding it leads to lying to people you care about . . . well. Sometimes that leads to even more conflict in the long run."

Mal thought about yesterday and hugged her pillow.

"I know how it is," Dad said. "Making things worse." He hesitated, then added, "I tried to talk to you about that the other night, actually."

Mal frowned. "When we had pizza?"

Dad nodded. "You were kind of off in your own headspace. But I wanted to apologize. For what happened at Thanksgiving. I'm sorry."

Oh. Mal looked up at him, realization dawning.

"Did Gran-Gran talk to you?" Mal asked.

He raised his eyebrows. "You think my mom told me to say I'm sorry?"

Mal shrugged.

"Okay," Dad admitted, grinning self-consciously. "Gran-Gran did talk to me. And I'm glad she did. I really am sorry, Mallory. I agree with you completely about that kiss at the parade being completely acceptable and a beautiful example of two people loving each other."

"Yeah, it was," Mal said. "And I tried to say so."

"You did. And I just brushed you off," Dad said.

Mal frowned. A stubborn, hurt part of her remembered Dad shaking his head and sending her out of the room. "You shut me down," she said quietly.

Dad winced and rubbed his forehead. "I . . . yeah. I guess I did. It wasn't right of me." He looked miserable. "I'm proud of you, you know? For speaking up? I'm glad you didn't just let it go. And I should have told Marie and Todd what I thought, especially when I saw it was important to you."

"Even if it meant conflict?" Mal asked.

"Even if it meant conflict," he agreed. "I've been working on that. Facing hard things." Dad's face was set in a determined look. He nodded and repeated, "I can do hard things." It sounded like something he had practiced saying. Like something to hold on to. *I can do hard things.*

Mal's lip quivered. "I don't really like hard things."

"Oh, Pumpkin. Come here." He wrapped her in a hug while Mal cried some more. She wasn't sure how there were still tears in her.

When she finally stopped, he rubbed her back and said, "So, you finally got mad, huh?"

"It was bad. I really screwed up." Mal gripped the quilt in her fists and sniffed. "I'm such a terrible person! I never should have said all that—"

"No, you're not." Her dad scratched his chin. He needed to shave, and Mal remembered that he'd just gotten back from a business trip. "You just have . . . feelings. And you can't bottle them up."

Mal raised her eyebrows. Her dad never talked about feelings.

He gave her an embarrassed smile. "I've been going to therapy," he said. "Learning about . . . expressing anger and being who I am and all that."

"And facing hard things?" Mal asked.

"And that." He nodded. "It might help you too. Learning to express your feelings. Express who you are."

Mal frowned. Being who she was had made everything worse. If she had just kept on being who everyone wanted her to be, none of this would have happened.

"I wish I could just undo everything," she mumbled. "I don't know what to say to Mom."

Dad nodded thoughtfully. "Why don't you write it out?"

He shrugged. "Maybe it'll be easier on paper."

"Is that what you do? Does that help?" she asked.

He let out a deep breath and nodded. "I'm trying. I think this kind of thing takes practice. But you need to start somewhere."

Mal meant to write an apology to Mom. But her mind was still a jumble and drawing felt easier. She took pictures of her new sketchbook pages, even the one the boys had folded and scrunched. Then she started tracing over the lines on her iPad, inking the edges and adding in shading. By the time Mom got home, Mal had nearly finished a new episode. Her mind felt calm again.

Mom seemed uneasy. She edged into Mal's room, eyeing her like she didn't know her own daughter anymore. Mal felt the guilt rising in her throat at the sight of her. Mal wanted to talk to her like Dad had said. But all she could manage was another tearful "I'm sorry."

Her mom took a deep breath. "We need to talk, Mallory." Mom sat down next to Mal's bed and looked at her with worried eyes. "I'm not sure what's going on. But I need you to be honest with me. None of this is like you. Skipping swim. Not turning in schoolwork."

Mal looked up at that and her mom nodded grimly. "I got an email from Mrs. Secant about your math homework. You are in danger of failing a class?" Mom shook her head in disbelief. "Some of your other teachers seem concerned too. Miss Hill tells me she had to give you an extension on your art project. And the way you blew up yesterday . . . I just don't understand, Mallory." Mom's lips tightened into a thin line. "I called the library."

Mal gulped.

"While I am glad to know that you have actually been volunteering, I still don't understand why you would be secretive about it. They were under the impression that I knew. Apparently I emailed them?" Mom's face flashed with anger and Mal recoiled.

"I'm sorry, Mom—"

Mom reached for Mal's Chromebook. "I assume that was on here?" Her voice was cold as she opened the Chromebook. Mal swallowed hard, watching her mom open the browser and go to her email. Her password filled automatically, and Mom let out an angry huff when her inbox opened.

"Mom, I'm really, really sorry," Mal said, her eyes watering again. "I was going to tell you, but then I was afraid you'd say no and I didn't want you to think I was trying to get out of swimming."

"But you were." Mom frowned. "Can you at least tell me why?"

Mal opened her mouth, then closed it. How could she explain? None of her reasons made sense anymore. She looked down and shook her head no.

Mom sighed. "Well, until you get your math caught up, you won't be going anywhere. I've told them not to expect you at the library for a while." She frowned at the screen, typing as she talked. "I would confiscate this, but I need you to use it for homework. I am logging out and changing my email password, though." Mom turned her eyes on Mal. "I need you to understand, Mallory," she said in a voice that made Mal feel like she was on the witness stand. "Impersonating someone else is a very serious offense. I'm sure it didn't feel that way when you did it, but it is considered fraud."

Mal's mouth went dry. "I . . . broke the law?"

Mom nodded. "I don't want you even to consider doing something like that again, understand?"

Mal nodded, the tears spilling over in silent trickles down her cheeks.

Mom suddenly looked very tired. "I need to go in to work tomorrow and finish up some things from yesterday. Your dad has agreed to watch the boys. For a few hours." Her mom's face tightened. Mal was sure she was remembering what Mal had yelled about not being her nanny. She shrank against her pillow. "Anyway, you should have plenty of time to get homework done." Mom stood up. "Focus on math. We'll talk about swim later." She gave Mal a sad smile as she left the room.

Even though Mal had already decided there was no way she could go through with the drag queen story time, a hard rock sank into her belly and settled at the bottom. She was grounded. Noa would be there tomorrow, expecting Mal. Counting on her.

Mal reached for her phone. She still hadn't said anything to Noa. But this wasn't something that would just go away. She had to tell them. She started typing, then deleted it. She tried two more times before finally texting.

Mal: I'm sorry. I'm grounded. I can't come.

That was it. That was the truth. At least the very basics of it. Noa couldn't be mad at her for that, right? She waited for a moment, but there was no response. Mal had to start on her math, she knew that. But her mind was on Noa. She checked her phone every few minutes as she tried to work.

Her phone buzzed, and she jumped for it. But it wasn't Noa.

K.K.: You sick today?

Mal bit her lip. She didn't know what to say. Maybe she could just pretend nothing had happened.

Mal: stomach bug

K.K.: sure, Dr.BotGirl.

Well, that didn't work. Her friends weren't going to let her pretend nothing had happened. Mal felt her eyes water.

Mal: I'm sorry. Does everyone hate me?

K.K.: define everyone.

Mal: do you?

K.K.: Tell me something Mal, all those times we

did our makeup together did you just think I was some kind of shallow princess or something?

Mal groaned and dropped the phone on the bed. Of course K.K. was upset. Everyone had misinterpreted her character as superficial and looks-obsessed. That was not at all the point of Linda. She rubbed her hands over her face and picked up the phone again.

Mal: That's not it at all! You don't understand.

K.K.: So tell me.

Mal licked her lips. Everyone already knew about *Metal-Plated Heart*. Hiding anything at this point would only hurt the people she cared about even more. So Mal told K.K. She explained how smart Linda is and how she teaches other people confidence. She told K.K. to read episode eleven, where Linda organizes the laborers in an uprising to demand fair treatment. Most important, Mal apologized for hurting K.K. She sent text after text, in a long string. Each one felt a little bit easier than the last. Finally, she stopped, waiting to see what K.K. would say.

K.K.: Thanks for telling me all that.

Mal let out a breath. That was something at least.

Mal: Do you forgive me?

K.K.: I'm trying to decide. Why didn't you tell me before?

Mal: It's hard to explain. I just didn't want everyone at school reading my comic.

K.K.: Well, too late for that. Everyone knows about it.

Mal: Everyone???

K.K.: Most people don't know it's you. But yeah. Brett found out about that one episode and got all mad so now everyone is reading it.

Mal dove for her Chromebook and opened Comic Koala. Thirty-two new notifications. Most of the comments were on the episode about the evil alien election. The new followers were Brett and his friends, she was sure of it. She scrolled through the comments and then wished she hadn't.

What sad toddler drew that spaceship?

This face looks like a tomato

Is this supposed to have an actual plot? Im so bored.

It's like a nerd party on this site!!! Look at all you nerds! Get a life!

She swallowed hard. Negative comments didn't last on Comic Koala, but unless there were bad words in them, the bots couldn't detect them. Once the admin saw them, they'd be removed. Whoever posted them might even get their accounts suspended. But she doubted they cared about that. They had probably only got on to make fun of her in the first place. They probably weren't even thirteen. Although neither was she.

Her phone buzzed again.

K.K.: you need to talk to everyone else.

Mal: I'm sorry. Tell everyone I'm sorry.

K.K.: tell them yourself

Mal groaned. It was starting to sound like she might need to apologize to the entire universe. But after talking to K.K., it felt like a bit of weight had lifted. Just a tiny bit. She still had hurt Wendy and Etta and her mom and her brothers. And Noa. She'd let so many people down. But just that one honest apology had loosened part of the tangled knot inside her. Her dad had said it might be easier to write things out. Maybe he was right. She bit her lip and opened her email.

This time she wrote to Mom. At first the words were awkward, and she just kept repeating, "I'm sorry." But then it felt like it had when she was making her self-portrait. She just kept telling one piece at a time, putting it all together until the whole mess was on the page. She told her Mom how she felt about swim and why. She told her how much she wanted to help her but how sometimes she wanted some time by herself. She told her how the twins made her brain feel like it was going to explode sometimes. She admitted she was behind in her homework, and how hard math was for her. Being honest with Mom had seemed so impossible when she was sitting right in front of her. But writing it out was easier.

It was late when she finished. Everyone else in the house was asleep. Mal emailed her apology to Mom, knowing she wouldn't see it until morning. She should have been exhausted after all that had poured out of her. But Mal felt wide awake. *I guess sleeping all day will do that,* she thought wryly.

After struggling through all the math she could handle, Mal tiptoed downstairs and dug through the cabinet of crafting supplies. If she was going to write a gloomy, heartfelt apology to Noa for totally standing them up, she may as well try to make it look good. Mal pulled out some drawing paper, colored pencils, and glue. At the back of the cabinet, she spotted a giant ziplock bag of glitter, leftover from some old project. Glitter seemed appropriate for a card for Noa. She tugged it out and added it to the rest.

Making something helped take her mind off things, and Mal slipped into the kind of fog that she would sometimes lose herself in while making comics. When she finished, the front of the card had a drawing of a teary-eyed girl with a word bubble that said "SORRY" in glitter letters. She'd tried to make the face look like hers, but somehow it ended up looking more like Zee's. It would have to do. She'd let it dry and then figure out how to get it to Noa tomorrow.

By now it was past midnight and Mal was finally ready to sleep. But when she got to her room, Mal noticed a voicemail notification on her phone. It was from Noa. They must have called while Mal was downstairs. Mal's breath caught, and she tapped the voicemail.

"Okay, so, I'm pretty mad. You didn't even text me yesterday. Also, I talked to Etta. And she was pretty skeptical that you were

into theater. So that was weird. I don't know what is up. Everyone has, like, a totally different picture of you and, like, . . ."

Noa's voice fell. They sounded tired. *"Look, Mal, I tried to be someone I wasn't for a long time. So I know what it's like. But I hope you don't think you need to do that around me. Anyway, I was really calling to tell you that the drag queen story time is canceled."* Noa sounded choked up now. *"The guy from the senate called the library board and they decided to cancel it. So, don't worry about missing it tomorrow. That's all. Bye, Mal."*

Chapter Twenty-One

Comic Koala Direct Message

To: Dr.BotGirl

From: S.J.theBoss

I want you to know that our admin has deleted comments on some of your episodes and disabled several accounts for violating our terms of conduct. We will continue to monitor the comments and do all we can to keep this space safe and welcoming. I am committed to standing up to anyone seeking to put others down, and I am sorry that some of them found your comic. Thank you for sharing your creativity on Comic Koala and I hope you continue!

Also, I'm still hoping your parent or guardian will contact me, Dr.BotGirl. I'd love to have your participation in our comic workshop.

Write on,

S.J. Summerhill

She/They

Being awake while everyone else in the house was deep in dreamland gave Mal a strange, disconnected sense. She kept thinking about Noa, who knew exactly who they were and who loved their labels. Noa, who got it that Mal didn't want to fit herself into a box. Noa, who wanted so much to share the drag queen story time with other kids who might not know there were different ways to be. And all those people who had taken that away from them.

It was pointless. She couldn't sleep. She ended up on Comic Koala, reading the message from S.J. Summerhill. It was a relief that the bad comments were gone now. But worry twisted in her belly. She still hadn't responded to S.J. Summerhill's message about the workshop. But how could she without losing her whole Comic Koala account? Although that didn't seem quite as important as it had just a week ago. Before all of this. Before she had messed up in so many ways.

Then Mal had a thought so startling and perfect that she

snapped her Chromebook shut and stared at it. Her brain usually moved slow, processing things one at a time. But now it raced.

She heard the words from all S.J. Summerhill's messages in her mind. *"We need more creators willing to stand up to hate."* *"You've created quite a fun, inclusive world." "I am committed to standing up to anyone seeking to put others down."*

She heard Noa's choked voice in the message. *"They decided to cancel it."*

She pictured the little boy who loved *Pinkalicious* and Etta's little sister, Lola, in her dress-up clothes, waiting for the drag queen story time that would never come.

She thought of the Comic Koala shop and its side door that opened onto the brick patio. She thought of the bar next door that never used the patio until later in the day and the twinkle lights that draped the fence and trees around it. And S.J. Summerhill, the mysterious owner who she had never seen but who, surprisingly, had somehow turned into her biggest fan. Mal smiled. Slowly, as if afraid of scaring herself off, Mal opened her Chromebook.

Her mind was moving slower now, mulling things over. As she opened a new message and started typing, a nagging little voice reminded her that the website would close her account if they knew she was only twelve. Her parents would probably triple ground her. She hesitated, her fingers hovering over the keyboard. If she did this, people would find out about

Dr.BotGirl. People at the library and at school. Not just her friends either. Brett and P.J. and the kids who had left mean comments. Mal's body tensed at the thought of all of them mad at her. Then something her dad had said popped into her mind. *I can do hard things.* Mal took a deep breath and typed, "I have a favor to ask."

As she wrote, the voice reminded her of all the reasons why she hadn't told her friends about her webcomic. But she gritted her teeth and kept typing. Mallory Marsh had been hiding for a long time. It had seemed easier. It had seemed like that was what everyone else wanted. But she pictured Noa and Shuga Toast and Davey and Lola and she let her heart pour out in what might be her very last message ever to S.J. Summerhill.

On Saturday morning Mal jerked awake to a commotion downstairs. It sounded like the boys had gotten up to something again and Mom was yelling at them. Mal rubbed her eyes and then remembered the message she had sent late last night. Well, early this morning, actually. She dove for her Chromebook and opened it up, certain there wouldn't be anything. It was probably too last-minute to ask anyway. S.J. Summerhill wouldn't have responded in time.

She was wrong.

Mal read the new message with a smile that grew and grew. She typed a quick response, then jumped out of bed, excited for the first time in days to get up. She had a plan, but she was going to need help. And she was going to need her mom to unground her, just for today. She hurried downstairs to find her mother standing in the living room with her arms full of colored paper, pencils, and glue.

"Good morning," Mom said. She wore an expression that was not exactly cheerful. "Your brothers got up first today, as usual. And apparently, they found all of this waiting for them." She nodded her head down at the things in her arms.

"Oh," Mal said slowly.

"And," Mom said, nodding to the carpet at her feet, "this."

Mal followed her gaze to a mound of pink glitter. A twinkling circle spread out around it, dusting the carpet with sparkle. Half buried at the epicenter she could see the glistening remains of the ziplock bag.

"I'm sorry, Mom!" Mal said. It seemed like all she could do lately was apologize. "It was late and I left it out."

"Oh, you aren't the one who decided to 'see what happens when you jump on a glitter balloon,'" Mom said with an exasperated look. "I sent them out back to play while I clean it up. I think our carpet is going to have glitter in it for months. Even after I vacuum."

"I'll vacuum, Mom," Mal said quickly. She hurried over and took the things from her mom's arms. This was not the time to ask Mom if she could please not be grounded anymore. "I'll put this all away too. I should have last night."

Her mom smiled gratefully. "Thank you," she said. "I'd like to get some real clothes on. I'll be back down in a moment."

Mal was kneeling on the floor, putting the last of the pencils back in the craft cabinet behind the table, when she heard the back door open. She peeked up in time to see Winston poke his head inside and look around. He turned over his shoulder and whispered loudly, "It's okay! They're gone!"

Wyatt followed him inside, walking, surprisingly. In fact, it was more of a shuffle. And he was carrying something. Something furry and squirming.

"Oh my gods!" Mal said, leaping to her feet.

Wyatt jumped in surprise and dropped the cat. It fled in a streak of white and caramel, disappearing under the couch.

"Mal!" Wyatt yelled. "You scared our kitty!"

Winston dropped to his knees by the couch. He put his mouth to the space underneath and said, "Sorry, kitty. Please come out, kitty!"

"Wyatt, she is definitely not our kitty. Someone lost her."

"But, Mal!" Wyatt said. "We were gonna hide the kitty!"

Winston looked up at her seriously and nodded. "We can keep the kitty secret and feed her tuna sandwiches and milk and hide her in the basement so Mom doesn't say no and she can be ours forever."

Mal looked at Winston's earnest little face and Wyatt's determined one and sighed. It was always so hard to say no to them. But she couldn't pretend like this would work. If she didn't explain this now, it would only hurt them more later.

"That cat belongs to someone," she said. "Remember the posters we saw? We'll have to go look at them and get the phone number to call. Actually, I bet I can find their number if I search the neighborhood app."

"No!" Wyatt ran over to her and pulled at her arm. "Please don't look it up!"

Winston scrambled to his feet and ran over to Mal, throwing his arms around her. "We promise we'll be good and not make you mad anymore, Mal-Mal!"

Mal's heart clenched. She looked down at the twins. "I'm really sorry for saying those things," she said. "I didn't mean it. I like playing with you guys, even if you get kind of loud sometimes." She winced. "But it's not your fault I got mad. I shouldn't have let it all build up like that. I love you guys. You are the absolute best little brothers." Mal ruffled their hair, and they grinned up at her. "But," she added, "that doesn't mean we can keep the cat."

"Cat?" Mom asked, coming down the stairs. "What cat?"

At that moment the cat slipped gracefully out from under the couch. Everyone stared as the pink nose sniffed the air and the little white-and-caramel paws stepped cautiously along the carpet. Even with her fur matted and a bit of cobweb caught in her whiskers, Mal recognized the adorable cat from the poster.

"That cat," Mal said.

"Wh—that—" Mom stammered.

And then the cat lowered her fluffy body onto the pile of glitter in the middle of the carpet and rolled over. She batted her paws at the air, flipped to her side, then rolled back over. The pink glitter clung to her fur, coating her white fluff in sparkle, but she kept on rolling.

"By all the goddesses," Mom murmured.

The cat was not a fan of vacuums. Her response to theirs was a Glitter Cat rampage around the house. The mini explosion the boys had left on the carpet earlier was nothing compared to the glittering, sparkling film that had settled over every inch of the downstairs by the time Mal had the cat safely in her arms. Mom vacuumed the site of the explosion, then looked around the room despairingly, as if wondering if it would be worth trying to vacuum the table and the TV stand as well.

"We have to get this cat out of here," Mom said to Mal. "I need to get to work and your dad is coming and . . ." She trailed off, rubbing at her temples.

"I know exactly where to take it!" Mal said. "Listen, Mom, I know I'm grounded, but the event that I've been helping with at the library is today. Wait," she said when Mom started to argue. "Hear me out. Please. I know where the Lost Cat posters are, and there are some in the library lobby.

I can get the number, and I bet the person will want to come right away. The library is a good safe place to meet someone. And then I can help out with the event. I can leave right now, and you won't even have to worry about it. Please, Mom?" She looked down at the glittering cat she was holding against her glittering shirt. "I'm already covered in glitter. I promise, when I get home I'll help clean up the house. But right now, you are so right. We have to get this cat out of here."

Mom looked at Mal and let out a long sigh. She looked around the house and at the glitter that seemed to cover every inch and sighed again. "I guess that does make sense. I really can't deal with this cat right now, and I doubt your father—"

"Thank you, Mom!" Mal said. "Just hold her for one second, okay?" She pushed the cat at mom and hurried upstairs to grab her phone. She had to text Noa. And the rest of comic club. And Etta and Wendy and probably K.K. and Yasmin too. She needed all the help she could get. Behind her, she could hear Glitter Cat purring loudly. It was a shimmery, hopeful sound.

Chapter Twenty-Two

MAL PULLED HER BLUE PUFFER COAT AROUND HER and adjusted the straps of her ripped backpack as best she could. She was wearing it on her front and upside down, with Glitter Cat inside so her head could poke out through the ripped seam. The zipper was held shut with a zip tie and Mal had stuffed an old scarf in to form a cushion. It was not exactly comfortable for Mal, but the cat seemed fine with it. It was warmer than it had been all week, but it was still the first day of December. The poor cat seemed content to snuggle in close to Mal's warmth and let someone else take charge. She purred the whole four blocks from her house to the library. Mal was fairly certain that cats were not allowed inside. She was also fairly certain she would be able to evade the security guard long enough to get to Zachary with her important news, but she wanted Noa to be there when she did. So Mal stood in a patch of morning sunlight outside the library while Glitter Cat purred and rubbed her whiskered cheeks against the zippered edge of Mal's coat.

She didn't have long to wait. Noa came around the corner, their wool coat buttoned all the way up to their chin and a knit cap covering most of their curls. They walked with a slump and they looked strangely colorless, like they were under a sepia filter. Mal felt her heart leap and ache at the same time. Noa stopped and took in Mal and her sparkling coat.

"Hi," Mal said. "Thanks for meeting me."

"Hi," Noa said. Then after a thoughtful pause they said, "Why is that cat covered in glitter?"

"Oh," Mal said. "Because I made you a card, but the boys spilled the glitter." She started to reach for the card, but the cat wriggled when she shifted it.

"Um, actually, can I give it to you later? Basically the cat was my excuse to come here, even though I'm grounded. I need to find one of those posters and call her owner, but there's something really important that I need to do first."

Noa looked at her curiously.

Mal swallowed hard. "Noa, I'm really, really sorry. I shouldn't have bailed on you. The truth is . . ." She took a breath. "I don't do stuff like that. Performances, I mean. I get really weird about being in front of people. At first I just kept pretending the lip sync was a fun thing I could do just with you, but this week it started to feel real. And with people talking about protesting the event too . . . I knew I couldn't go through with it and I kind of shut down."

Noa looked down at their shoes. Their hands were in their coat pockets, and with the buttons all done up, they looked closed up tight. "Why didn't you tell me, then?" they said to the ground.

"I should have, definitely," Mal said. "But I was scared."

Noa looked up at that, their eyes gray and uncertain. "Scared of me?"

"N-noooo," Mal said, looking away.

The cat squirmed. She realized she was squeezing her arms around the backpack and loosened her grip. Mal felt ridiculous, like she was someone in a show saying melodramatic lines. But it was real. It was more real than all the different shades she had painted herself for so long to so many people. This was how she felt. "I didn't want our practices to stop. So I tried to be someone you would want to be with. I know that is messed up, but I just . . . didn't want to lose . . . that." She whispered the last part, looking down at Glitter Cat.

For a moment the rattling hum of the cat's purring was the only sound in the air.

Then Noa spoke softly. "I don't want to lose you either. But honestly . . ." They let out a frustrated breath. "I'm just not always sure who you are. You're one thing with me and another with other people. I mean, you don't even know what pizza you like!"

"What?" Mal asked in surprise. "Sure I do."

"Okay, what's your favorite pizza at Pizza Pundit? And do not say the Rachel just because you know I like it!"

Mal swallowed. She *had* been about to say the Rachel.

"Fiona said the Jake is your favorite," Noa said, their eyes narrowing. "Your brothers told me you like the Van, same as them. And Etta says you always get the Thomas when you're with her. So? Which one is it?"

Thinking fast, Mal said the name of the only pizza that none of her friends ever ordered. "The Tucker! The Tucker is my favorite."

Noa's eyes widened. "Mal, the Tucker is *no one's* favorite. It isn't even a pizza! It's dough. The description on the menu literally says"—they did air quotes around the words—"'just a ball of dough.' You buy it to make your own at home!"

"Fine!" Mal ducked her head. She felt like she might cry. "I—I don't really know. I just go along with other people because I don't usually care that much what we eat, and I want other people to be happy."

"Okay," Noa said. They looked straight at her and nodded. "Thanks for admitting that. And"—they shrugged—"wanting other people to be happy isn't the worst reason for not being yourself. It sucks that you pretended to be into theater just for me, though. I mean, I had fun with you. But we probably could have had fun together anyway, even without that. And yeah, you should have told me sooner. But thanks for telling me now."

Mal nodded. It wasn't exactly an epic love scene. Noa was definitely still hurt and not too sure if Mal could be trusted. But it was a start.

"So," Noa said, "why are we meeting here?"

"Oh," Mal said, feeling a rush of excitement. "Right. Will you come in with me and talk to Zachary?"

Noa looked surprised but nodded. Mal pulled the coat closer around her Glitter Cat backpack, and together, the three of them entered the library.

"So, what does the cat have to do with this?" Zachary asked.

The security guard would have kicked them out immediately when he saw the cat's head poking out of the backpack, but Mal had convinced Zachary that what she had to say couldn't wait. He had ushered them into his office and stood there now in his button-up shirt and tie, looking confused.

"Oh, nothing," Mal said, scratching the cat's head with

one sparkling finger. "She's just . . . along for the ride?" Now that she was here, she felt strangely nervous, almost as if there were an audience instead of just Noa and the library manager. "It's about the drag queen story time."

A cloud passed over Zachary's usually composed face. He opened his mouth, but Mal hurried on.

"I know they made you cancel it. But I have an idea. Do you know Comic Koala? The comic shop down the street?"

Zachary nodded slowly.

"The owner, S.J. Summerhill, wants to host the story time."

Mal waited, trying not to look at Noa. She had no idea what Zachary would say or if Shuga Toast would even go for this. Maybe Mal shouldn't have asked Noa to come. Maybe this would just be another disappointment.

Zachary was frowning. "At the comic shop? There's not really space in there for a crowd."

"Not inside, but the bar next door has a great patio that connects to their yard. They don't open until later and they said S.J. could use it. And they have outdoor heaters, even though it's not that cold today."

"But we already sent out a notice that today's event was canceled—" he began, but Mallory cut him off.

"You just sent that out last night, right? Not everyone will see that. People are still going to show up for it. And there were flyers posted around the neighborhood that are still up. People will come, I know they will. We should have something for them when they do."

Mal heard an intake of breath from Noa, but she still didn't look at them.

Zachary's gaze had drifted, and he seemed to be thinking this through. "I don't know if we can get it figured out in time," he said. "The story time was supposed to be at eleven thirty. That's in two hours."

"We can help make more signs," Mal said. "To spread the word. I already asked some people to come help." She wasn't sure if everyone she had texted would actually show up, but she had to try.

Noa nodded eagerly. "I'll help too," they said.

"And I can give you the owner's number," Mal said. "S.J. Summerhill. She already said it's okay, but she wants to talk to you about it. She's expecting you to call."

"You know her?" Zachary asked. "She is fully aware of what this is and what's been going on?"

"Well, I sort of know her," Mal corrected. "I haven't met her in person." She didn't tell them that one of the things S.J. Summerhill had requested was for Mal to come to the story time so they could finally meet in person. "But yes, she knows all about the story time and Shuga Toast. And she knows about the protestors," Mal added. "But since you already technically canceled it, she thinks we probably won't have anyone show up to protest. And you wouldn't be going against the library board either."

"All we'd be doing was directing people to go somewhere else," Zachary mused. "It would certainly work if Shuga Toast is in. And no one on the board could complain since we wouldn't be hosting." He sighed and his shoulders sank. "I just wish we could really stand behind this in a bigger way. As a library, I mean."

"First of all, Shuga Toast *is* in!" came a voice from the doorway. They all turned to see a light-skinned Black man in a leopard-print hoodie. He stepped into the office with one smooth, graceful movement, crossed his arms, and leaned his head back to look at Mal. "Girl, you are just sparkling today."

"Oh," Mal exclaimed as she recognized his face. "You're Shuga Toast!"

"Yes, sometimes. At the moment, I'm Anthony." He lifted his carefully penciled eyebrows at her. "Nice cat. Love the glitter." Then he smiled at Noa. "Noa!" He wiggled his fingers in a wave. "Good to see you again!"

"Hi, Anthony!" Noa grinned. Their eyes were brighter than they had been when they met Mal outside, and she felt that glimmer of hope again. Maybe things would be okay after all.

"And second," Anthony said, turning to Zachary. "If you want to stand with this whole shindig, Zach darling, then let's give it some pizzazz." He gave a wide, white smile. "How far is that comic shop? Two, three blocks?"

Mal nodded.

"Well, then, a fabulous musical parade sounds right up my alley. We gather our story time crowd in the courtyard out front and pied-piper them off to the new location." He wriggled his fingers through the air as if he were scattering pixie dust. His fingernails were spectacularly long with sparkling designs painted in gold. "If they don't want us in here, baby, let's take it to the streets."

Not only was the story time back on, but now they had added a parade. Anthony had a trunk full of Shuga Toast's stuff he'd left here the day before. He'd come in to pick it up this morning after the cancellation, but with the story time back on, he disappeared into the restroom to transform into Shuga Toast. Lucy had a paper crown and wand craft she was setting up in the kids' area and several little kids were already well into making their own for the parade. Mal checked her messages. The comic club kids were on their way. She hadn't heard from her other friends, and her heart sank. But Noa was in high spirits. They headed out to corral all the staff the library could spare to accompany the crowd to the comic shop. When Mal tried to follow Noa out the staff door, Zachary waved her back.

"I'm afraid you really can't have the cat out there," he said. "You'll need to take it home."

"I am *trying* to get her home," Mal explained. "I just need to find her owner."

Zachary tilted his head. He looked closer at the cat in Mal's backpack and said quietly, "Well, would you look at that?" Before Mal could wonder what he meant, he opened the door and called out, "Barbara! Come here, please!"

A moment later, Barbara stepped into the staff room, her expression stern. "Young man, you may be the manager, but there's no need for you to raise your voice like that. This is a library."

Zachary grinned and raised his hand, gesturing toward Mal. He looked very pleased with himself.

Barbara's eyes met Mal's and then her gaze took in the cat, glimmering with pink sparkles in its white-and-caramel fur. Her mouth dropped open.

"Fluffernutter?" Barbara whispered. She stepped closer to Mal and fumbled for her glasses where they hung on her pearled chain. She pushed them up her nose and peered at the cat. "Fluffernutter," she said again. Barbara reached out her arms and Glitter Cat scrambled out of the hole in the backpack toward her. Barbara gathered her against her chest, glitter and all.

Mal watched in amazement as tears fell quietly down Barbara's pale cheeks and Barbara scratched the furry ears. Fluffernutter purred in satisfaction.

"Why don't you take a break for a bit?" Zachary told her

gently. "I'll cover the desk."

Mal started to follow him out the door, but Barbara stopped her. "Wait, please." Her voice was softer than Mal had ever heard. "Come sit with me a moment. I'd like to hear how you found my Fluffernutter."

It was surprisingly easy to talk to Barbara. She kept a candy dish in her office and insisted Mal take as many as she wanted. Barbara laughed out loud when Mal described the twins' antics and the glitter situation. Barbara closed the office door so Fluffernutter could explore, and the cat sniffed each corner of the room carefully, leaving traces of glitter here and there. Mal even showed Barbara the card she had made for Noa, with the glittering "Sorry" across the front. They both laughed when Fluffernutter sniffed the card and immediately sneezed.

"I hope your cat isn't sneezing glitter all over your house for days," Mal said.

"I suppose my house needs a bit of sparkle." Barbara said. She looked at the card, then at Mal with her sharp eyes. "I hope your friend forgives you."

"They already have mostly," Mal said. "But . . . Well, I'm not sure they're ready to really trust me again."

"Why's that?"

"I just . . ." Mal paused, thinking about how to explain. "I wasn't honest, I guess. About who I am. I was afraid they wouldn't like me if I was myself."

"Hmm," Barbara said. Then she reached for a framed quote on her desk and handed it to Mal.

"If I didn't define myself, I would be crunched into other people's fantasies for me and eaten alive."—Audre Lorde

"I saw this before," Mal said. "On that paper you gave me."

Barbara nodded. "There will always be people with their own ideas of who you should be," she said. "And that can eat you up if you let it." Barbara glanced at Fluffernutter, who was curled in the corner like a pink sugar donut. Barbara's face softened. For the first time, Mal thought that maybe it wasn't so much stern as sad. "It took me a long time to figure that out. People still do try to define me. As too strict or mean. Some even call me Barbara the Brutal." She looked sideways at Mal.

Mal sucked in her breath. "Or," she said cautiously, "how about Barbara the Benevolent?"

Barbara opened her mouth and let out a laugh. She shook her head, her eyeglass chain swinging. "I've certainly never heard that one before." She chuckled.

There was a knock on the door, and Noa poked their head in. "Mal, did you text the whole comic club? Because they're here and they want to help!"

As Mal slipped out of the office, Barbara forced a pocketful of candy and a twenty-dollar bill on her as a reward for finding Fluffernutter. Noa was waiting, decked out in the tangerine tutu and platinum wig from their practices, grinning a thousand-watt smile.

"Shuga Toast has a portable speaker, and Lucy is going to sing her number while we walk," they said, the words tumbling out. "And my moms are coming with my sibling. Will you wear your costume? You don't have to perform at all, and if you don't want to wear it that's fine, but also, it's a fur, so you might want to because it's cold—"

Mal waved her hands to stop the words, laughing. "Yes, I'll wear it. And here, this is for you." She handed Noa her apology card.

"Wow!" Noa stared at the drawing on the front. The girl who was supposed to be Mal but looked more like Zee stared up at them. "Did you draw this?" they asked.

Mal nodded, embarrassed.

"This is so good!"

"Not really," Mal insisted. "It's pretty basic. I've just done a lot of that comic style, I guess, so it turned out okay."

Noa tilted their head, their eyes narrowing as they examined the drawing closer. "You've drawn this before?" they asked. Then their eyes widened. "Wait, this is from that webcomic!"

"Yeah!" Marcus was suddenly standing next to them, leaning over Noa's shoulder. "That's Zee," he said, in an excited voice that cracked a bit. "From *Metal-Plated Heart*!"

The smile wavered on Mal's face as she looked from him to James and Izzy. "Hey," she said. "You guys came."

"Course." Izzy shrugged. "You asked us to."

The matter-of-fact way she said it made Mal feel a startled kind of happy. Like a pocket full of candy from someone you didn't expect to like. She looked at each of them and licked her lips. "I need to tell you guys something. About Dr.BotGirl."

Marcus nodded, Izzy narrowed her eyes, and Noa leaned forward. Mal took a deep breath. "It's me."

For a split second they were silent. Then Marcus let out a whoop and lifted a fist in the air. "I knew it!"

Izzy's eyes widened. "No. Frikkin. Way."

"Wait, you are?" Noa said, staring at Mal. "You made *Metal-Plated Heart*? For real?"

A slow smile spread across James's face, and he nodded at Mal.

"If you're Dr.BotGirl," Marcus said, gaping at her, "that means you are one of the top amateur illustrators on Comic Koala."

"Why didn't you tell me?" Izzy said, grabbing Mal's arm. "I had no idea you were that good!"

Mal ducked her head, flushing with pleasure and embarrassment.

Marcus was staring at her in awe. "You might win the competition for best amateur comic artist! You have a ton of followers!"

"Over three thousand followers," James said.

"Yes!" Marcus whooped again. "We have Dr.BotGirl in our comic club! That is awesome!"

"Nice," Izzy said.

"Well, I don't know if I will still be Dr.BotGirl anymore," Mal muttered. "Not after this." Her throat felt suddenly tight.

"What do you mean?" Noa asked.

"Well . . ." Mal stopped, not sure she wanted to admit it out loud.

"Ohhhhh," Marcus said, his voice hushed. "You lied about how old you are, right?"

"She lied about a lot of things," said another voice.

Mal looked up to see Etta, Wendy, Yasmin, and K.K. walking toward her.

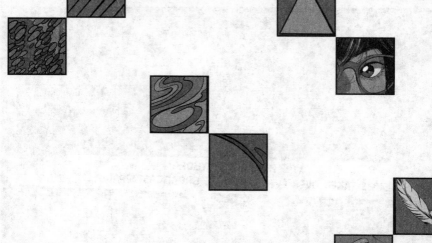

Chapter Twenty-Three

"HI," MALLORY SAID. IT CAME OUT IN A SQUEAK.

Etta crossed her arms over her oversized purple sweatshirt with "Love Is Love" splashed in rainbow colors across the front. She frowned, Etta-fierce. "So, you wanted to talk to us?"

"I'm sorry," Mal blurted out. "I should have told you sooner. I didn't want you to be mad and I didn't want you to see my notes and I never wanted you to get hurt. I wasn't trying to be mean or anything with the robots, I promise. Smoker is actually amazing, and Tack is a complete genius. Opie is such a good friend and Linda—" Mal looked at K.K., trying to discern something under her frown. Had K.K. forgiven her yet? "Anyway, I'm sorry if I hurt your feelings." Mal made herself stop talking and breathe.

Noa looked at them all, a confused expression on their face. "Wait, Smoker and Opie the robots? And Tack and Linda? Like, from the comic?"

"Yeah," Etta answered, without taking her eyes off Mal. "Mal turned us into characters in her comic."

Mal cringed, and Marcus croaked, "Seriously?"

And then Izzy and Noa both said, "That is so cool," while Mal cried out, "I'm so sorry!" at the same time.

Wendy raised her eyebrows at Mal. "We aren't mad about that."

"What?" Mal asked.

Etta threw her arms out to the sides. "Mal, we're mad that you didn't tell us! I'm fine with being a robot!"

"You . . . are?" Mal asked.

"Again," Noa said, "for the record, I think it's super cool."

"Yeah," Marcus said, bouncing up and down. "You guys are famous!"

"I mean, I didn't really love the episode where Tack almost screws everything up," Wendy said slowly, tugging at her braid. "But, yeah, most of them are actually really cool."

"Tack *doesn't* screw up, though!" Mal jumped in. "Because of Smoker." She looked at Etta, her eyes pleading. She needed her friends to understand this. "Smoker is the one who jump-starts Tack when Tack is stuck in processing mode. Because that's you two. You're both so important. You see? And when Smoker goes off without a plan, Tack is the one who brings her back!"

"I mean, that really is you two," Yasmin said.

"Mmmhmm," K.K. agreed, raising one eyebrow. "What's your latest thing called? Operation Warm?"

Wendy and Etta looked at each other. Etta snorted and Wendy giggled.

"Okay, I guess it is us," Wendy agreed.

"Operation Warm?" Mal asked.

"Wendy helped me figure out an idea for converting unused buildings in the city to emergency winter shelters," Etta explained. "My mom is going to bring it up at her next meeting with the church leaders."

"We named it Operation Warm," Wendy said. She smiled at Etta. "We do make a great team."

"Yeah, we do. And honestly, I love Smoker," Etta said. "Even if she does get stuck racing in circles sometimes. She totally makes up for it with her Everything Generator. Smoker can do anything!" Etta struck a fierce pose.

Izzy was staring at Etta, her eyes wide. "You are Smoker?" she said. "Smoker is my favorite."

"I like Opie," James said, his eyes on the ground. Mal could have sworn his cheeks turned pink.

Yasmin looked surprised. Then she frowned at Mal. "I'm

not sure Mal does," she said.

"Are you kidding," Mal said. "Opie is Zee's best friend. She's always there for her and the whole team. She's so thoughtful and kind."

"Just not honest about how she feels?" Yasmin asked. Her mouth twisted like she'd tasted something sour. "And she's super passive-aggressive?"

Everything in Mal wanted to assure Yasmin that she was wrong. She wanted to convince her that she'd misread the whole thing and that Opie wasn't that way at all. But Mal was being brave now and being honest herself was one of the bravest things she could do.

"I just think you could say how you feel more," Mal said quietly, looking at the ground. "I don't ever know if you are annoyed with me or something."

"Well," Yasmin said, taking a deep breath. "How about this? I am annoyed with you, Mallory Marsh."

Mal lifted her eyes, a little afraid of what she would see. But Yasmin just shook her head and smiled. "I mean, look who's talking about not being honest, though."

Etta yelled, "Whoa, passive-aggressive burn!" and everyone, even Mal, burst out laughing.

K.K. elbowed Mal and said, "I'm not mad anymore. Linda is actually the greatest of all time. Her mini-revolution is inspiring." Mal looked at her in surprise and K.K. nodded. "I read the whole thing. You were right."

"So you guys really aren't mad about . . . being in my comic?" Mal asked in a small voice.

"I mean, it's a little awkward," Wendy said. "And you shouldn't have lied to us."

"Yeah," Etta said. "You could have told us, Mal!"

Mal swallowed. "Yeah, I could have. I *should* have. You guys are all really good friends, and I should have let you know about that part of myself. I'm sorry."

"Honestly, as soon as people started reading it, we were going to figure it out," Etta said, sounding exasperated. "We know you, Mallory Marsh. You are the only one who could possibly have been Dr. BotGirl."

Mal took a long shuddering breath. She smiled. "So, if everyone is done being mad at me, want to help throw a drag story time?"

James, Marcus, Izzy, and Mal got to work making signs to direct people to Comic Koala for the story time. Wendy got her older brother and his friends to help her distribute them around the neighborhood. Crack o' Dawn Café put one in their window and Fat Marv took down the Lost Cat poster to make room for one on his bulletin board in Pizza Pundit. Etta started a word-of-mouth campaign, spreading the news through her mom's connections to families with little kids. Yasmin helped Lucy in the kids' area and Noa rushed around in a happy frenzy, foisting costumes on anyone who was up for it.

Mal felt different around her friends. Now that they had all read her comic, it felt as if they knew everything about her. It was unsettling but not exactly bad. And they had shown up for her, even after all that had happened.

The story time was supposed to start at eleven thirty but for the first fifteen minutes it was just an impromptu dance party in the courtyard. Lucy, in a poofy yellow dress with a hem of frothy lace, danced with kids waving colorful ribbons. Noa handled the playlist and encouraged everyone to do different silly dances. To her surprise, Mal saw Barbara come out of the library and stand near the back, swaying to the music with Fluffernutter in an actual cat carrier backpack. It looked way more comfortable than Mal's old backpack. Etta's sister, Lola, wore an Elsa dress, a superhero cape, and a smile that seemed too big for her tiny face. Mal had texted her dad to come too, but she wasn't sure if he would. Sometimes getting anywhere with the boys was just too much of a hassle. Finally, Zachary took the portable microphone. He gave a quick announcement, explaining exactly where the comic shop was and reviewing some safety tips for walking there. He was careful to explain that the library was not hosting this event and that Shuga Toast would be taking over from here on. Mal knew he was planning on staying behind to answer any phone calls that might come in about whether they were in compliance with the library board. He'd seemed disappointed not to come, but he'd also told her that not all fights happen in the streets. Mal liked the thought of that.

"And so, lemons and jelly beans," Zachary said, "without further ado—"

"What?" Mal laughed. "Did he say lemons and jelly beans?"

Noa clapped their hand over their mouth, giggling loudly. "He asked me what he could say that was less gendered than 'ladies and gentlemen' and I gave him this whole list of things but wow. Lemons and jelly beans? I'm pretty sure he just made that up."

Zachary continued over the giggles in the crowd, "—our own remarkable local queen, Shuga Toast!"

Everyone cheered, and Shuga Toast herself danced up to the front. She wore a shimmering silk dress with a dusting of white glitter across the top that looked just like crystalized sugar. Her wig was magnificent, sleek and huge, an elaborate updo with loops and curls around the sides. Every time she moved, the sunlight glinted off another part of her costume. This was so much better than being inside, Mal thought. The sun showed off Shuga Toast way better than fluorescent lighting could. Shuga Toast welcomed everyone, showed the kids how she could twirl on her sparkling high heels and then, with the crowd following and the music playing, paraded down the sidewalk toward the comic shop.

The cars along Main Street slowed down to wave and honk. There was one car with a driver who yelled out something angry, but with the music and the singing no one could tell what he said. Some people walking by on the sidewalk asked where they were going and joined in. Zachary had let Lucy and Barbara leave early, along with a couple other library staff members who were marching with the crowd.

"Hey," Noa said, falling into step with Mal and linking their arm in hers. "So you put all your friends into your comic. But who in your comic is Mallory Marsh?"

"Oh," Mal said, embarrassed. "No one. I'm just writing it."

"What about Zee?"

"No," Mal said, shaking her head. "Zee is the best parts of all my friends. She fights for justice like Etta and thinks before she acts like Wendy. She's kind like Yasmin and a great leader like K.K. I even gave her Wendy's braid and Etta's bracelets. And Zee's ship is a turtle because K.K. likes turtles, and Zee's favorite color is pink just like Yasmin." She shook her head again. "Zee's them, not me."

"But that's why Zee *is* you," Noa said. "Zee brings everyone together. Just like you."

Mal raised her eyebrows doubtfully, but Noa waved an arm at the crowd. "I mean, look around us. Zee couldn't have done a better job."

Mal looked around. There was a dad with a little kid on his shoulders and a mom pulling two toddlers in princess dresses in a red wagon. Noa's moms and little sibling were all marching, waving rainbow flags and singing along. Barbara and Glitter Cat and Lucy were there. James, Marcus, and Izzy managed to argue while marching, and Yasmin had joined them. Etta had linked arms with Wendy and K.K. and was trying to get them to do some complicated dance steps.

Mal smiled. Noa was right. The naysayers and the Ohio Senate and the library board couldn't stop them now. She had figured it out. She had found a solution. She *was* like Zee. Mal felt invincible. Then she suddenly remembered that they were about to walk up to Comic Koala. She was about to meet S.J. Summerhill. Dr.BotGirl would not be anonymous any longer. Her webcomic would be put on hold until she turned thirteen, and even then, S.J. could say she had violated terms of use and not allow her to come back. Mal's steps slowed.

And at that very moment, the playlist switched to the next song.

"Okay, can I just say something crazy?" Anna's voice rang out over the speaker. Noa looked at Mal and their cheek dimpled. They stepped away and reached back toward Mal, their brown hand with its purple fingernails open and waiting in the fresh December air. Mal put her hand in Noa's and felt a shiver run through her. As the music started, Mal slipped automatically into her part, following the lifeline of Noa's warm hand. Some of the kids nearby pointed and clapped and a lot of people sang along with them. It was nothing at all like performing onstage. Mal laughed and danced. By the

end of the song, Shuga Toast had arrived at Comic Koala, the whole crowd in tow behind her.

Mal could see a tall, brown-skinned woman in a woolen poncho waving them toward the side patio. S.J. Summerhill was older than she'd expected, with white streaks in her straight black hair. As everyone else crowded onto the patio, Mal pulled Noa to face her.

"Noa?" she said, her voice shaking. "I'm not really into labels and all that. But I think I'm whatever label means I like you." She wanted to sink into the ground as soon as the words left her mouth.

Noa gave an embarrassed laugh. "I mean," they said, looking at their shoes, "maybe you're bi or pan? But, really, Mal, it's fine if you don't want to label yourself one thing or another. Labels aren't always great. I mean, that's kind of why I love drag. It's a way to mess with labels, you know? And I think," Noa said, their dimple deepening, "if you wrote *Metal-Plated Heart*, then I have a pretty good idea of who you are." Noa leaned closer, their eyes as deep and blue-gray as the ocean. "The real you," they said. "And I like you just for you."

Mal wasn't entirely sure she knew the difference between bisexual and pansexual. She'd have to look that up later. For now, Noa's last words blocked out everything else. *I like you just for you.* Despite the cold, Mal felt warmth all the way to her toes.

The story time was a huge success. After all the complaints and publicity, more people showed up than they had expected. Shuga Toast ended everything with a round of the Hokey Pokey. When they got to "put your whole self in," one of the moms picked up her toddler and swung him forward. He kicked his tiny feet and shrieked with joy as she twirled him around.

"Yeah, little buddy!" Shuga Toast cheered. "Your whole self is itty-bitty but you sure got a lot to say!" She clapped her hands and looked around at the smiling crowd. "Now I want you all to remember, my friends, that every bit of you is precious. Your right arm and your left arm." She did the motions as she said each part. "Your right foot and your left foot." Noa grinning, stomped their feet along with Shuga Toast's sparkling heels. "And your whole beautiful self!" Shuga Toast called out, throwing her hands in the air and jumping forward. All the kids jumped forward along with her. Noa threw their hands wide, letting out a "woo-hoo" as they did a little shimmy.

Shuga Toast raised her voice and called over the laughter, "Every part of you is precious and welcome. Keep on reading and keep on showing up with your whole self! I love you all! Bye-bye now!" She waved and blew kisses as they all applauded. Noa cheered loudly and rushed over to talk to Shuga Toast. Mal watched them go. She couldn't stop smiling. Shuga Toast's words rang through her head. *Every part of you is precious.*

"So, this is what you have been up to?"

Mal whirled around. Her mom stood behind her in yoga pants, a black jacket, and a checkered scarf. It was her "power woman on the weekend" look, and she was staring at the crowd with an expression Mal couldn't read.

"I thought you were at work," Mal said.

"I finished up quicker than I expected. And your dad said you'd texted that the boys might enjoy this. So I decided to bring them." Mom glanced over to a table where the twins were making something sparkly with Lucy. "Why does everything today seem to involve glitter?" she wondered aloud.

Mal threw her arms around her mom. "I'm really glad you came," she said into her mom's jacket. "I know I was just supposed to return the cat, but this was really, really important to me."

Her mom's arms tightened around her. She kissed the top of Mal's head and said, "I know. Your email explained quite a lot." Mom pulled away and looked at her. Mal felt herself blushing. So much had happened since she'd written that email. She wasn't entirely sure she remembered everything she'd said to her mom.

"Mallory," her mom said. "It was . . . I'm . . ." Her mom paused, and Mal realized with a start that her mother, her practically-a-lawyer mom, was at a loss for words. "Thank you," Mom said finally. "For sharing yourself with me." She reached out a hand and smoothed Mal's messy hair. "My darling, I wish you'd talked to me about all of this. You have been carrying so much. And I"—she swallowed—"I've been adding to it without realizing."

Mal wanted to insist that it was fine and she hadn't really meant it. Maybe then they could all pretend things were back to normal and everyone was happy. But was that the most important thing?

"We have a lot to talk about," Mom said. "But first, there's someone else here waiting to speak with you." She leveled a stern look at Mallory. "She apparently knows you by a different name. Doctor somebody?"

"Dr.BotGirl," someone said, stepping forward, and Mallory's heart sank.

Chapter Twenty-Four

THE WOMAN'S VOICE SOUNDED WARM, LIKE A
pebble left in the sun. She even looked a bit like a rock, her
broad shoulders draped with a dark gray poncho and her
black hair streaked with white.

"S.J.theBoss?" Mal asked in a small voice.

S.J. let out a chuckle. "I think we're past usernames. You
can call me S.J."

"The library manager was kind enough to put us in touch,"
Mom said. "S.J. is one of the reasons I decided to come today.
It seemed about time for us to have a chat."

Mal looked back and forth between her mom and S.J.

Summerhill. *A chat?*

S.J. cleared her throat. "I don't often host events, Mallory. This one has been lovely, even if I did only agree to it as a favor to a comic artist I know." She raised an eyebrow at Mal. "But now I'd like to know why you have been avoiding me ever since you arrived."

Mal gulped. *I can do hard things*, she thought.

Mallory started with her first registration, when she was just figuring out the webcomic site and posting random drawings. Then she explained how she got her idea for *Metal-Plated Heart* and started a new account under the name Dr.BotGirl. And she admitted that she had lied about her age way back when she first started posting. Her mom and S.J. both listened, waiting until she was done. Then S.J. Summerhill nodded slowly and seriously.

"I appreciate your talent. But this will mean suspending your account, Mallory. Much as it disappoints me to do so. At least until you turn thirteen."

"But," Mal stammered, "what about the competition? The votes?"

S.J.'s eyebrows dipped. "*Metal-Plated Heart* is no longer eligible, Mallory. Comic Koala does not reward dishonesty. Did you truly think there would not be repercussions?"

Mal's shoulders slumped. For so long, it had felt like lying was the easiest solution to things. She'd started to think she could just rewrite her life by saying what she wanted to be true even if it wasn't. But in the end, it had made everything so much worse. "No," she whispered. "I guess not."

"And after you are thirteen, it will still depend on your mom." S.J. added.

Mom nodded in agreement. "We will have to have a conversation about that, Mallory," Mom said seriously. "I'll be talking to your dad too. Regardless of why you did it, you have been deceiving us for a long time. We'll need to work on some boundaries to rebuild trust before you create any other online accounts."

Mal felt herself sink even more. S.J. noticed her expression.

"Building trust is very important, Mallory. With your parents and with me. Otherwise they may not agree to let you work with me."

Mal lifted her head. She pushed her glasses up her nose and stared at the older woman. S.J. smiled down at her.

"You truly do have talent, Mallory. I don't often work with artists as young as you, but if you are interested and your parents approve, I may be able to show you a few things about comic design."

Mal began nodding her head aggressively before S.J. even finished speaking. "Yes!" she said. "Definitely, please yes!"

S.J. smiled at that and nodded her head. "Very well. As much as I have enjoyed corresponding with Dr.BotGirl, I look forward to getting a message from Mallory Marsh very soon."

A white blur streaked past Mal, clawing its way up S.J.'s poncho. S.J. stumbled back and looked down at the cat, who was hissing and cowering against her chest. Mal looked up to see Wyatt and Winston barreling toward them.

"Not this again," Mom said, rubbing her temple.

Mal cut the twins off. "Leave the kitty alone, you two!"

She could see Barbara making her way through the crowd. Just a few days ago, Mal would have thought she was furious. But now she saw the worry drawing Barbara's face tight. Mal turned to her brothers.

"This kitty is really important to Miss Barbara," she said seriously. "Really important. Like the way that Archie is important to Gran-Gran. And here, with all these people, the kitty can get scared easily."

"But I was gonna keep her safe!" Winston said.

Mom knelt, coming down to the twins' eye level. "Let the grown-ups keep her safe, okay?"

"Why?" Wyatt demanded. "I can hold a kitty."

Mal had seen her brothers hold the cat, the way their arms crossed over the fluffy body awkwardly and they leaned back to keep her from sliding to the floor. Mom must have been thinking the same thing, because she reached for the boys' hands and stood up.

"How about if the people the kitty already knows hold her, okay?" she said, leading them away.

"Do you know the kitty?" Wyatt demanded, tilting his

head back to look up at S.J. The woman looked uncomfortable. She glanced around as if hoping help would arrive. And then it did.

"Oh goodness, thank you. I thought I had lost her again," Barbara said, scooping the cat from S.J.'s arms. "She doesn't usually react that way to noise, but she's been through a lot lately." The librarian looked at the comic shop owner's dark poncho that was now sprinkled with pink glitter and white cat hair. "Oh. Oh my." Barbara started rummaging in her bag. "I have a pet hair roller somewhere."

S.J. put a hand on Barbara's arm. "It's quite all right, love." She gave Barbara a closer look. The librarian's usually neat gray hair was mussed, and her coat was covered in glitter. She'd pushed her glasses on top of her head, and one end of the chain had detached from the frame and was tangled in her earring. "You look as if you could use a moment of quiet. Would you like to sit inside for a bit? There is a back room where your cat can settle down away from all this commotion."

And Barbara, the always-fierce, always-put-together librarian, smiled at S.J. and nodded a yes, ducking her head so low that her chin touched the cat's fur. *Barbara the Bashful*, Mal thought with surprise. They walked together toward the side entrance of the Comic Koala and S.J. opened the door for Barbara and Fluffernutter.

"Mallory," her mom said, touching her on the shoulder.

Mal turned. The boys had gotten distracted by James and Marcus, who were sitting at a table and drawing cartoon animals for the kids crowding around them. Mal looked at her mom, suddenly afraid of what was coming.

"I'm so sorry, Mom!" she said. "I completely blew up at everyone the other day. I'm a terrible person!" Mal squeezed her eyes shut.

"Oh honey," her mom said. "You are not a terrible person."

"I am!" Mal's throat was tight. "I yelled at Wyatt and I scared Winston. What kind of sister does that? And I yelled at you. I know I hurt you, Mom! I—I'm so sorry!"

"Mallory, look at me," her mom said. Mal did, and her mom put one hand to her cheek. "You are my daughter, and you are the absolute best one I have."

Mal was her mom's *only* daughter, but their usual little joke didn't seem that funny right now. "I'm a mess," Mal mumbled. "I'm just a patchwork of what everyone else thinks."

Mom frowned. "What do you mean?"

Mal rubbed the back of her hand across her eyes. "Like my self-portrait," she said. "Just random patches of things."

Mom's eyes narrowed and then cleared. "Ohhh," she said. "Oh honey. If that art project I saw in your room was you, then it was beautiful and multifaceted, not a mess. If anything, it should have had *more* layers! Because you are not just one thing. I should know." Mom waved a hand toward herself. "I know what it means to have complicated layers, Mallory.

Sometimes it feels easiest just to fit inside the simple black-and-white lines people draw for you. But you are much more than one box or one label, Mallory Marsh." Her mom traced the tears leaking down Mal's cheek.

Mal threw her arms around her mom and held on tight. "I didn't mean it, Mom. What I yelled at you."

"Well," her mom said seriously, rubbing Mal's back, "after what you said in that email, I think you meant at least some of it."

Mal pulled back, biting her lip. She looked at her mom in her perfect clothes and she took a deep breath. "Y-yeah, maybe I did mean some of it."

Mom nodded. "There may have been a better way to bring it up, but . . . you were right. I need to do better at listening to you. I didn't ask you about the schedule. Not really. I know how much you love to swim, and you've done team for years so I just assumed you would want to."

"No, I'm sorry, Mom! I should have said—"

"Do you hate swimming?" her mom asked.

Mal hesitated. "Well, no, I do love to swim. . . ."

"But do you hate team?" her mom asked.

Slowly Mal nodded. Her mom gave one sharp nod back. "Okay."

"Okay?" Mal asked, disbelief fighting with hope inside her. "Just okay?"

Her mom sighed. "You do not need to stay on the team.

I'll admit, I liked the idea of it. It's really the only physical exercise you get regularly, and I thought the discipline would be good for you. But the main reason I signed you up was for you. Because I thought you loved it."

The relief won out and Mal felt her shoulders loosen. "I *do* love to swim, Mom. Because the world just drifts away in the pool. I don't have to listen to all the noise. But competing isn't like that at all. It's all about what's around you and being better or faster than whoever's next to you. And Coach Perkins . . ." She didn't want to say more but Mom gave her a knowing look.

"He's not exactly the peaceful type, is he?" Mom asked. Mal shook her head no. "Well," Mom said, "I can understand why you've been miserable. But why didn't you tell me instead of skipping?"

"I didn't want you to be disappointed in me," Mal said, looking at her feet. The front of her coat still shimmered with leftover glitter, and she brushed at it helplessly. "You were so excited for me, and I just didn't want you to worry. And I thought if everything was going really well, then . . ." Mal's voice dropped. "You wouldn't make us move to Sacramento."

Mom stared at her. "Move? What are you . . . ?" She frowned. "Did you overhear a conversation you weren't meant to?"

Mal shrugged miserably, and her mom's mouth tightened. "Just because Emo Sue and Halmoni suggest something doesn't mean I'm going to do it. You should know your mother makes her own choices." Mom let out an annoyed huff. "I'm perfectly happy here."

"But you've been sad more since the divorce," Mal said. "I thought that if you got too sad here, you might want to leave. And I just wanted to make it all okay here. I wanted you to be happy."

"Well," her mom said with one of her quick, decisive nods. "I think the moral here, at least partly, is that we should all stop assuming we know what will make other people happy, right?" She raised one eyebrow at Mal. "After all," she added, "I was making choices that I thought would make you happy. Although I suppose they also seemed like the easy solutions to things."

"I'm sorry!" Mal said, for what felt like the millionth time. "I don't want to make everything harder on everyone!"

Mom held up a hand to stop her, the way she did when she was in a conversation or on the phone. But this time she was focused entirely on Mallory. "Listen to me, Mallory Marsh. Even if it were easier for you to do things exactly as I thought they should be done, even if it were easier for you to be just like me, that would never be what's best. No matter what lines other people draw for you to fit inside, you are you. And I want you to be exactly who you are. In full color."

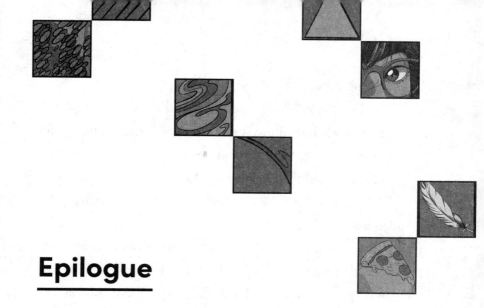

Epilogue

THE LATE DECEMBER WIND WAS BLOWING HARD as Mal climbed from the minivan and waved goodbye to Noa. She slid the dented van door closed and ran up the steps to her dad's apartment, balancing the pizza boxes on one arm as she turned the doorknob.

"Whoa, kiddo, let me give you hand." Her dad grabbed the boxes and set them on the table while Mal shrugged off her new backpack and coat. "You didn't walk, did you? I told you I could pick you up."

"I got a ride with Noa," Mal said, slipping off her shoes. "Their mom was picking them up at the library anyway, and they didn't mind waiting for the pizza."

The boys raced down the stairs and hurtled toward the pizza, roaring like lions. Or dinosaurs? Mal grabbed the smaller box before they could get to it.

"This one's mine!" she said quickly.

"What? No fair!" Wyatt yelled. As an afterthought he added a ferocious growl.

"I paid for it with my own money from the comic shop," Mal told him. She glanced at Dad, who smiled and gave her a respectful nod. Mal still couldn't believe S.J. let her take tips. Even if they weren't a real paycheck, it felt good to have her own earnings. Wyatt still looked mutinous, so Mal added, "You wouldn't want it anyway. There are mushrooms in there."

Wyatt made a face and went back to the double pepperoni.

"Can I eat upstairs?" Mal asked Dad.

"Yeah, sure," Dad said, sliding a plate under Winston's droopy slice of pizza a second before it dripped onto the table. "But your math homework is priority! Promise you'll do that as soon as you finish eating?"

"Promise!"

In her room, Mal set the box on her desk and dropped her backpack. It thudded to the floor but not too hard. After talking it over with her mom, Mal had asked Wendy if she could keep her project supplies in the science room so Mal would have space in her locker again. She still liked being the person her friends relied on for things, but she'd started keeping most of her stuff in her locker. She didn't want to rip another backpack. She'd also asked Yasmin for her calculator back. It hadn't fixed Mal's issues in math, but it had definitely helped.

A crashing sound came from downstairs. It sounded like someone had leaned their chair back too far from the table. Mal felt her body tense, but then she forced her shoulders away from her ears and took a deep breath. She didn't need to go down there. After lots of discussion and scheduling, her parents had settled on a new routine. On the nights Mom worked late, the kids went to Dad's. Mal still watched her brothers now and then, but most of her afternoons were free to focus on homework. She was also allowed to spend time at the library and the comic shop, as long as she stayed caught up in school.

A loud and familiar wail started downstairs, and Mal reached for her noise-canceling headphones. After Mal had explained about how much she loved the peacefulness of being underwater, Mom had surprised her with these. The hug of the soft cushions around her ears instantly cut down on all the sound around her. Mal tapped her phone and heard the relaxing sound of a gentle rainfall. She smiled up at the wall where she'd hung her patchwork self-portrait from art class, along with the framed Audre Lorde quote Barbara had given her and a bulletin board covered with Polaroid pictures. Noa laughing while they tried to juggle. The whole comic club on their field trip to Comic Koala. Noa and Mal peeking around shelves in the library. Mal and Etta holding a banner with the rest of the GSA that said, "You are beautiful. You are worthy." Winston and Wyatt showing off the manicures Mal had given them.

She opened the pizza box and took a deep breath. The smell of the flavors mingled in the steam like different shades on a piece of art. Fat Marv hadn't batted an eye when she asked him if he could give her a little taste of each one. He'd just said, "One sampler, comin' right up." But when he'd handed her the box, he'd held on to it for just a moment and said, "You make sure and tell me which one you like best, okay, Miss Mallory?"

Mallory knew that her brothers loved the Van and Noa loved the Rachel. Etta liked the Thomas, Wendy preferred the Roger, and Fiona always ordered the Jake. Mal knew what everyone loved, except for Mallory. Time to change that, she thought, and reached for a slice.

Author's Note

In many ways, this book is a celebration—of queerness, drag queens, libraries, nerdy fangirls, cyborg revolutionaries, and even a glitter cat. But it is also a celebration of our own messy identities.

For some, like me, it takes until we are quite grown to define ourselves. Although my family was incredibly loving, they raised me within straight, unyielding, heteronormative lines. Terms like *bisexual* (attracted to more than one gender) and *pansexual* (attracted to all genders) were not in my vocabulary. Even now, after learning those words and recognizing myself in them, I tend to use the more general term *queer* (a word that covers a spectrum of LGBTQIA+ identities and orientations) to describe myself. I have met so many wonderful people over the years—my friends, my children's friends, library customers, readers of my books, and kids in the schools that I visit—who identify as *nonbinary* (not exclusively a boy or a girl). Some use the term *enby* and they/them pronouns, like Noa. Some do not. But every single one of them is precious and there will always be space for them in my life.

When I wrote the world around Mallory Marsh, I wanted her to have every opportunity to try on different identities and to be whoever she wanted to be. I hope each of you reading this book has that kind of safe, accepting space. If you don't have that right now, please know that it is out there. I hope, with all my heart, that you find it sooner rather than later. And if you still don't know what to write on your sticky name tag, just know that this universe contains a whole rainbow of different shades. You'll find your colors.

Acknowledgments

In 2021 I sat in a room with other library staff at the Ohio Library Council Convention and listened to Nick Tepe (director of the Athens County Public Libraries) talk about saving a drag queen story time. Thank you, Nick, not only for taking the time to fan that spark of a story by answering all my research questions, but also for your years of advocacy for justice and inclusion in our libraries. You taught me that not all fights happen in the streets.

My brilliant agent, Brent Taylor, took my glimmer of an idea and came back with a two-book deal. Like some kind of magician. Thank you, Brent.

My editor, Jennifer Ung, continually amazes me with how thoughtfully and thoroughly she engages with these characters I made up. Thank you for loving my Rooville kids as much as I do, and for reminding me, yet again, of the power of nuance.

Thank you to Maine Diaz for the incredible interior illustrations. When I wrote a book character who wrote her own webcomic characters I had no idea I would get to see those characters come to life. Maine's remarkable talent has left me in happy tears again and again. Thank you, Maine, for reading my script and somehow knowing exactly what Zee looks like. Thank you for turning Rattletrap into a turtle and making Dubs way cuter than I could have imagined. You would win the Comic Koala competition, hands down.

Carolina Fuenmayor, thank you for portraying Mallory so perfectly, surrounded by patchwork details and the colors of the pansexual flag. I'm honored to have your gorgeous art on another one of my book covers.

Thank you to the entire Quill Tree/HarperCollins team who brought Mallory's story to full color: Rosemary Brosnan, David DeWitt, David Curtis, Jon Howard, Robin Roy, Meghan Pettit, Liate Stehlik, Sabrina Abballe, Patty Rosati, Kerry Moynagh, and the Harper sales team, Tom Pombo and Laura Raps.

Tyler Littlejohn gave feedback on the Korean words and cultural references in this book and those moments are better because of him. Thank you, Tyler, for sharing your own experience and your intersecting identities with such grace and generosity.

My writing critique group, the Manuscribblers, read Mallory's story before anyone else and helped me find my way through the weeds back when it was still a NaNoWriMo mess of a book. Thank you. I'm so glad SCBWI brought us together.

Thank you to Laura Bontje and Leo Embry for reading my drafts in my various moments of panic and assuring me that it was, in fact, not hot garbage.

And Kelly Young and Heather Thompson-Gillis, who did that and so much more. My band, my crone coven, my Subpoena Potential, I love you both so much.

Thank you to my family most of all. My husband and partner, Matthew Leahy, has been with me every step of the way on my own journey of identity. My kids—Graciela, Mateo, and Rosali—are constant sources of inspiration and support. I love doing life with you all.

And to library staff everywhere, thank you. My colleagues at the Columbus Metropolitan Library, particularly the South High Branch, are some of the most dedicated, big-hearted, thoughtful, creative, quirky folks I know. Thank you for creating spaces where people of all ages can find themselves. Thank you for being "Open to All."